The
Cassandra Virus

K.V. Johansen

ORCA BOOK PUBLISHERS

Library and Archives Canada Cataloguing in Publication

Johansen, K.V. (Krista V.), 1968-
The Cassandra virus / K. V. Johansen.

ISBN 1-55143-497-0

I. Title.

PS8569.O2676C38 2006   jC813'.54   C2005-907449-3

Summary: When Jordan creates a computer program that communicates
with him via e-mail, he has no idea the havoc the program will create
for him and his friend Helen.

First published in the United States, 2006
Library of Congress Control Number: 2005938207

Orca Book Publishers gratefully acknowledges the support for its publishing
programs provided by the following agencies: the Government of Canada
through the Book Publishing Industry Development Program (BPIDP), the
Canada Council for the Arts, and the British Columbia Arts Council.

Cover design: Lynn O'Rourke
Cover photography: Getty Images

Orca Book Publishers
PO Box 5626 STN. B
Victoria, BC Canada
V8R 6S4

Orca Book Publishers
PO Box 468
Custer, WA USA
98240-0468

Printed and bound in Canada
Printed on 100% recycled, old-growth forest free paper.
Processed chlorine-free using vegetable based inks.
09 08 07 06   • 5 4 3 2 1

for Norma and Ian,
since I borrowed their house
and their cats

I needed some technical advice on this one: Thanks to my cousin Amanda for reading an early draft of the story and commenting on computer-related matters, and to Chris, who gave me the initial idea, discussed the many drafts the story went through and provided numerous useful thoughts on technological innovations—*sine qua non*. Thanks also to Marina and Susanna, official test audience for this and other stories.

"This book reveals no state secrets."
—*An anonymous operative of an unnamed security agency*

Contents

Take One Bored Genius...

"Have you got it? Are you in yet?" Jordan's friend Helen leaned over from where she was playing a halfhearted game of computer Go. The computer was losing badly, which was usual. Helen was good at Go—better than Jordan was, in fact, even though he was supposed to be pretty much a genius at some things. Playing Go, as Helen never tired of pointing out to him, wasn't one of them.

"Almost," said Jordan, and then he was in.

He grinned, watching the blinking cursor in the plain, old-fashioned, text-based interface. No graphics here. This was the start-up for his sister Cassie's robot. Or at least its head.

INITIALIZE HEAD: Y/N?

Y

The screen of his laptop went dark for a moment, then blinked to life again. It showed a slightly crooked image of a very untidy shelf covered in odds and ends of hardware, and a concrete-block wall painted a thick, shiny, pale yellow.

"Oh," said Helen sarcastically. "A shelf. This is so, so exciting." Under the desk, her husky, Ajax, sighed deeply.

"What's exciting," Jordan pointed out, "is that I broke into Cassie's computer and turned the robot head's eyes on. I got through all her protections."

"Igor make good spy?"

"Igor make very good spy."

The screen went black again, and a white text message popped up:

Leave Baby alone, you Igor, and stay out of my files.

"Is she down in her robot lab?" Helen asked. "I thought I heard her talking to Mum in the office just a minute ago."

"It's an automatic response to someone hacking in," Jordan said. "I guess she figures nobody but me could do it." He was a little bit pleased about that, but a bit disappointed, too, that Cassie had been expecting him to try it.

"If I built a robot, or even a robot head, I'd name it something better than Baby," Helen muttered. "Igor bored, Igor. Igor vant to go do mad scientist stuff."

"Igor bored too. Igor think all Igors should—"

"The important thing is to reduce funding to any projects the university can't profit from right away. We need to leverage our research toward possibility." A man's voice came from the hallway, a sort of squeaky drone. "We need to be more efficient, more businesslike."

"Old Ruggles!" Jordan hissed.

Ajax growled. Helen poked him in the ribs with her toe.

"Quiet," she ordered in a whisper. "Are they coming this way?"

Tap tap tap. High heels echoed in the hall and grew louder. Jordan peered around the partition that gave people a bit of privacy while they worked. This wasn't a computer lab for regular students to use. It was the lab where Helen's mother, Dr. Naomi Chan-Fisher, head of the computer science department, worked with her graduate students on new codes and systems. Each of the powerful 128-bit processor workstations had its own screened-off cubicle.

Tap tap tap. High heels hammered on the tiling. They were definitely in the lab and coming closer, pausing at regular intervals as if peering into each cubicle.

Jordan nodded, whispering, "Yeah. Dormer and old Ruggles."

"We're trapped."

"Keep your head down. Maybe they'll think we're students if they just see our backs."

"Yeah, right," said Helen sarcastically. "Very short students." But she hunched over the keyboard, her long black hair making a curtain to hide her face.

Jordan logged off and shut down his laptop's wireless connection to the university network. Major trouble, if he got caught messing around with that. He shoved the laptop into his backpack and squeezed himself in beside Helen at the desk. She gave him the mouse and he switched the Go program to two-player mode, taking over the black game pieces. The aim of Go was to surround the other player's pieces and to capture territory. Great. From the look of it, he was losing before he started. What a waste of a powerful new computer, just playing games on it. There wasn't much else he was allowed to do, though. Dr. Chan-Fisher had told him very sternly not to alter any programs, not to write any programs, not to even look at the source code for any programs while he was in her lab. That was why he'd brought his own computer—playing games was boring.

Helen didn't much care about computing power one way or the other. She would rather have been out looking for salamanders in the old quarry, or at least doing some research on something she was interested in. However, even surfing the Web on university computers was forbidden to them since last Christmas, when Helen had ordered a dozen axolotls from an online supplier in California. It wasn't their fault that the computer science department's credit card number had been cached in the browser...Of course, it *was* their fault that they hadn't confessed what they'd done when the order Helen typed in as a joke had actually gone through. They couldn't hide it from Dr. Chan-Fisher when a dozen of the bizarre salamanders, with their big feathery fringes of gills, had been delivered to Helen's house. That was one of Dr. Chan-Fisher's more famous blowups.

Dr. Chan-Fisher had made certain Jordan and Helen paid the department back out of their allowances, but Helen got to keep the alien-looking axolotls. Jordan still felt miserable squirms of guilt whenever he looked at them, swimming happily in their huge aquarium, but Helen said he shouldn't blame the salamanders.

"...why does this computer need two monitors?" Old Ruggles or, more properly, Dr. Ruggles, one of the six vice-presidents of Muddphaug University, was coming closer. Vice-president in charge of snooping, nagging and penny-pinching, Jordan's sister Cassie called him.

No one answered him. He was talking to his skeleton-thin assistant, Ms. Dormer, who was always dressed in a color-coordinated business suit with a very short, tight skirt and high, high heels. Everyone loved Ms. Dormer's heels. They were as good as a bell on a cat.

"Make a note of it."

"*Yes*, Dr. Ruggles."

"And the door left propped open with nobody in

here. Who knows what could have gone missing? I want a memo sent to the department head. And—"

Dr. Ruggles and Ms. Dormer both stepped around the edge of the partition. Without meaning to, Jordan glanced up.

"Children!" The vice-president said it the way other people might say "Cockroaches!"

Ajax burst out from under the desk, barking. Dr. Ruggles yelped. Ms. Dormer clutched her handheld computer against her chest and scuttled backward, almost but not quite falling over.

Helen jumped up to grab Ajax by the collar, but the big gray husky weighed almost as much as she did. She couldn't hold him for long.

"Are you looking for Dr. Chan-Fisher, Dr. Ruggles?" Jordan asked politely. Helen never bothered to be polite, especially to people she disliked. "I think she just went to her office to get a cup of coffee."

"No food or drinks *allowed* in *computer* labs," said Ms. Dormer, and she wrote a little note on the screen of her handheld. She had an annoying way of talking in italics, like a bad actor, and she always wrinkled her nose up when she emphasized a word. It was hard not to start imitating her if you watched her for too long.

"The university is not a day care!" Dr. Ruggles said, his cheeks and his three chins quivering. He looked like a very ugly baby that someone had dressed up in a suit for a joke. "Dr. Chan-Fisher!"

Dr. Chan-Fisher's office was right next door. She came running in, leaving a trail of little coffee sloshes on the tiles.

"Dr. Fisher! This is a university, an institute of higher learning, not a day care! These children have no business playing in here. They could...could break something. *Things* could go missing."

"I beg your pardon," said Naomi Chan-Fisher, with her head a little on one side, like a bird. "Ajax, be quiet."

Ajax fell silent.

"Were you suggesting my daughter and her friend would steal...?" *Axolotls*, Jordan thought with a squirm. "No, I must have misheard. Don't mind Ajax. He's a very gentle dog really, but very protective of Helen."

"I've got a whole *computer* in my backpack," Helen muttered, wrinkling her nose at Jordan. "Wanna look?"

Jordan, who *did* have a whole computer in his backpack, kicked her ankle, not gently at all, and Dr. Chan-Fisher frowned sharply, but Ms. Dormer fixed a steely glare on Helen's backpack, which contained, Jordan knew, three field guides, two nets and assorted jars, all so far empty. So long as they didn't look in his...

"Why don't you two go play outside?" said Dr. Chan-Fisher. "Don't leave the campus."

"Keep that animal on a leash," said Dr. Ruggles. "And clean up after it."

"Dogs should *not* be allowed on campus," Ms. Dormer said. "After all, it *is* private property. Dr. Fisher, were you *aware* that university policy states all computer lab doors *must* be *locked* at *all times*? We installed automatic electronic *locks* for that very purpose. I sent out a *memo* only last *week, reminding* people in the computer science department that propping doors open is *strictly* forbidden by university *policy*."

"No one can reach this lab without walking past my office," Helen's mother was saying as Helen and Jordan tiptoed out, tugging Ajax after them. The husky followed reluctantly, giving the vice-president a very stern and disapproving look over his shoulder.

They passed a freckled, red-haired girl in the doorway—Jordan's sister Cassie. She was one of Dr. Chan-Fisher's graduate students and more or less a genius at things like languages, math and computers—which unfortunately were the same things Jordan was more or less a genius at too. She had learned Latin when she was five, begun studying classical Greek when she was six, and tackled Yucatec, a Mayan language, when she was seven. Their parents thought these were important and normal sorts of subjects for children to learn. She started on calculus, which is a tricky branch of math most people never need to learn at all, when she was ten. Jordan was six before *he* started Latin and nearly eight before he was really fluent in ancient Greek or in Yucatec. He started calculus when he was ten too, but still, that wasn't any *better* than Cassie. Everything he tried to do, everything he wanted to do, Cassie had already done, and it wasn't as if computer programming was even the thing she cared about most, the way it was for him. What she loved best was building machines and devices—she was brilliant at robots and engineering, while Jordan knew he wasn't much good at all when it came to that sort of thing. That made it even worse, because there wasn't anything at all he was best at. There just wasn't anything left. Sometimes he really wished he was the oldest so he could have gotten somewhere, *anywhere*, first, instead of feeling like he was running to catch up all the time, trying to overtake Cassie's ten-year head start.

And then he felt mean for feeling that way. It wasn't her fault she was born first, and she was his best friend other than Helen. For two-thirds of his life, she'd been his only friend. He gave her a grin. Cassie grimaced at him, hiding a cup of coffee behind her back.

"Computers are expensive and delicate pieces of equipment," Dr. Ruggles was explaining, as though maybe Dr. Chan-Fisher didn't know this. "They are not toys for irresponsible little children."

"Little!" muttered Helen in disgust.

"Irresponsible!" Jordan turned and stuck his tongue out at Ruggles's back. Dr. Chan-Fisher saw him and gave a sort of desperate, frog-like gulp as she tried not to laugh.

Jordan and Helen wandered across the campus, kicking the fluffy white seedheads off dandelions. It was the beginning of summer. School was over, not that school was very exciting or interesting. The teachers mostly ignored the bright kids. There wasn't much to do in the small town of Easter River in summer if you had just turned thirteen and weren't into team sports. Some years Jordan took university math classes once school was over, but he'd already done everything that was being offered in the summer session at Muddphaug this year. Boring. Jordan wished he was a grad student like Cassie, doing something important and interesting.

The reason they had to spend so much time being bored at the university was that Jordan's archeologist parents, Dr. Morris O'Blenis and Dr. Monique LeBlanc, were down in Belize in Central America, digging up the thousand-year-old ruins of a Mayan temple. Helen's father was dead, and her mother didn't like her staying alone at their big old house out at Wood Hill. The house looked down over the Tantramar Marshes, with its leaning old gray hay barns and, far away in the distance, the shortwave towers and the hypnotic turning of the white turbines of the wind farm. Beyond the dykes that kept the Marshes from flooding was the brick-colored water of the Bay of Fundy. Dr. Chan-Fisher was afraid that Helen, who was always poking around in ditches and streams and along the shore, would go out on the mudflats and get trapped by the tide. The red mud was almost like quicksand. Helen said she had better sense than to go out onto the mud-flats these days, but worrying about Helen was what Naomi Chan-Fisher did whenever she wasn't thinking about computers.

Helen was tall and what she called semi-Chinese, although she liked to point out she was also semi-Scottish, even if she didn't play bagpipes; she had dark eyes and long, straight black hair, of which she was secretly very proud. Jordan was still shorter than her (although Cassie assured him he would catch up soon), skinny and sandy-haired, with blue eyes. Jordan and Helen had become best friends in grade four, when Helen and her mother moved to Easter River. It had been so great suddenly not to be the only kid in the class who knew all the answers. He'd been able to stop feeling like such a freak. Igor and Igor, Jordan and Helen had started calling themselves—the hunchbacked assistants to the mad scientists. Although, just to bug Jordan, Helen always said computer programming wasn't a real science, not like biology or physics.

Leaving a trail of headless dandelions behind them, they wandered aimlessly from one interesting tree trunk to another, letting Ajax choose their route. He eventually decided one of the white pillars at the front of the adminstration building was the most interesting tree of all.

"How can one dog's bladder hold so much?" Jordan wondered aloud, looking up at the sky and feeling a bit embarrassed.

"He drinks a lot of water," Helen explained.

"Those children again! And that dog!"

They spun around guiltily. Ajax abandoned the pillar and lunged toward the vice-president, who was puffing along the path to the door, his face red.

"Jordan! Help!" Helen cried, and Jordan grabbed the leash too. It took both of them to pull Ajax back.

"*Defacing* university *property!*" Ms. Dormer twittered from behind the vice-president. "*Befouling* it!"

"The building won't melt," Helen snapped. "Anyway, it'll rain in a day or two. Ajax, heel!"

"C'mon, Ajax, heel," Jordan added, more of a plea than a command, and together they hurried off across the lawn again, tugging at the leash. Ajax kept watch over his shoulder and growled once or twice.

When they looked back as well, they could see Ruggles and Dormer still standing there, watching them go.

"He followed us. Old Ruggles followed us just to get Mum in trouble," Helen said indignantly.

"Oh come on, Helen. He must have better things to do."

"He likes getting people in trouble."

"What can he do? He can't fire her—I mean, she's a department head, after all."

"He'll do something," said Helen darkly. "Just you watch."

Add a Supercomputer...

Vice-President Ruggles did do something: He sent Dr. Chan-Fisher an e-mail saying children were not allowed in university buildings, and that if her vicious dog chased him once more, he would have it sent to the pound.

"That's ridiculous! There's no regulation that says you guys can't come into the buildings," Cassie told Jordan at supper that night, while a six-legged, solar-powered robot the size of a cracker bumbled about the table. Cassie had made a dozen or so little robots like it, trying out various designs over the years. Survival of the fittest, Jordan always said: the wimpy ones couldn't survive being used as cat toys. Cassie blocked the robot into a square made out of knives and forks, watching to see what it would do. "But Naomi thinks you'd both better stay away for a while. And make sure Helen keeps Ajax on his leash in town."

"Are we going to have a babysitter?" Jordan asked, picturing his whole summer disappearing. "It wasn't Helen's fault. Ajax hates Dr. Ruggles." Like any sensible creature, he added silently.

Cassie looked after Jordan whenever their parents were away on a dig. It was all right when he was at school most of the day, because she got home soon after he did, but in the summer she still had to be in the lab, working on projects for Dr. Chan-Fisher or on her thesis, which was the paper she was writing about her robot-head project.

"Naomi and I talked about it," Cassie said, putting her elbows on the table. The flat-bodied ant-bot pushed a gap between a knife and fork and escaped, heading for the edge of the table. Jordan caught it and let it go on the floor. "But we decided you and Helen were too old for babysitters. I mean, really, you're old enough to be babysitters." She grinned. "Not that I can think of anyone who'd hire you. Ooh, here baby, have a nice frog to play with..."

Jordan stuck out his tongue.

"So," Cassie went on, "we've decided you can stay here together. But you have to promise you won't hang around downtown, getting into trouble."

"Sure." As if the kids who hung out on the terrace in front of the bank would want him and Helen around anyway. This was far better than he had expected.

"And you aren't allowed to go to the quarry."

Jordan made a face. "Does Helen know that?"

"I'm sure Naomi'll make it clear."

Jordan was still in his pajamas the next morning when he heard gravel crunching in the driveway. He wandered out, munching toast, to see Dr. Chan-Fisher's little red truck sitting quietly in the yard.

"Cassie's already gone to the lab," he reported as Dr. Chan-Fisher helped Helen lift her bike out of the back. "Want a cup of tea?"

"Thanks, no, Jordan. I've got to get to work. Now Helen..." Dr. Chan-Fisher settled her glasses firmly on her nose and looked severe. "Are you listening? Stay away from the quarry."

"Yes, Mum."

"You've got your cell phone? You've got the lab phone number and the office number and my cell number in case there's any problem?"

"Yes, Mum."

"Don't go bike-riding on the highway."

"Yes, Mum."

"Keep Ajax on his leash, for goodness' sake."

"Yes, Mum. *Bye,* Mum."

Naomi Chan-Fisher gave her daughter a lopsided smile. "Have I forgotten anything?"

"Don't stick beans in my ears?" Helen suggested. "Don't run with scissors?"

Dr. Chan-Fisher rolled her eyes and gave Helen a quick peck on the top of her head before she hopped back into the truck. "Be good," she called, waving out the window as she drove away. The faint mechanical purring died away—it was a safety law that all fuel-cell vehicles had to have a noise added to their engines, because otherwise they were so quiet that people were always walking out in front of them.

"Hah hah hah," Jordan cackled, with his best mad scientist laugh. "Vhat shall ve do first, Igor?"

"Ve look for de eye of newt and toe of frog, first," said Helen.

"That's witches."

"Whatever. I'm going to the quarry."

"We're not allowed."

"Well, not the quarry. The stream that runs out of it. You can be Igor for me and carry my pail. Must have monsters for ze experimentz."

Jordan gave her a look.

"Vell, for ze aqvariumz."

"Um...but the stream...your mother."

"Mum didn't say to stay out of the stream," Helen said smugly. "So there."

"She meant..."

"Well, she didn't say it. Look, don't be such a wimp. I'm thirteen now, for Pete's sake. I'm not going to drown in a little stream that I can step over. Go put some clothes on. I don't want to be seen with an Igor wearing pajamas that have little yellow bulldozers on them. I don't even want to know you wear jammies with little yellow bulldozers."

"Grande-tante Thérèse," he explained. "You know what great-aunts are like."

"I do now. Hurry up. We're missing the best newting hours."

The quarry was in a forgotten wooded block of land at the end of a dead-end street halfway between the O'Blenis house and the campus. They spent the morning poking under rocks and fallen branches along the stream that ran out of it, although they found no newts. Anyway, Helen had a whole room out at Wood Hill full of tanks of newts, salamanders, toads and frogs. And, of course, the twelve Californian axolotls, with their feathery gills and surprised little eyes.

It was well after noon when Jordan finally persuaded Helen back to the house.

"Enough newting," he said over the sandwiches Cassie had left them for lunch. "There obviously aren't any newts around that stream, my sneakers are soaked and I think I've got a sunburn."

"Wimp. You're just going into computer withdrawal. It is possible to live for three hours without a computer, you know."

"It's not computer withdrawal."

"It is. You went to check your e-mail before you took off your wet shoes. I saw you. But fine, Igor can go sit in front of hypno-screen. This Igor go play by Igor-self. I'll go back to the stream."

"I think they want us to stay together. You know we get in so much less trouble that way..."

"It was you who said, hey, if you like those axolotls so much, why don't you order them?"

"Yes, well, I'm older and wiser now. Look, I spent all morning doing what you wanted, so can't you stick around here this afternoon?"

Helen stuck out her lower lip, not really pouting but pretending to.

"I suppose. If we're not good little kiddies we will get some sort of hideous babysitter, no matter how old we are."

"Very good, Igor. You get gold star."

"Igor yourself. What are you working on?"

"Stuff," Jordan said vaguely. It was hard to admit he didn't really have anything he wanted to do. Write another game? Last winter he had written a program for a game he called Ponkles, which was a silly strategy game. An army of cat-eared wizards tried to win control of a maze-like ruined city full of hidden items and unexpected booby-traps, while a bat-winged wizard army defended it. Ponkles II? No, that wasn't anything new and different. Design a new e-mail filter program to block out junk mail? Nothing seemed very interesting. His mind felt stale and tired. Those were both the sorts of things Cassie might do so easily if she wanted a break from working on her robot-head.

"A secret project?" Helen asked.

"Er, sort of."

Helen looked like she didn't quite believe him. "Hm. Igor look like mad scientist use Igor's last brain for window-putty. What's wrong?"

"Nothing!"

"If you say so. Want to play Go?"

"Not really."

"Fine. Go work on your secret project. I forgot to bring a book with me and I think I've read everything your parents have on Central American frogs. Maybe Ajax and I will just snoop around your house."

"Good. You can look for the missing robot."

"Which missing robot? It isn't one of those little ones that look like spiders, is it?"

"Igor not scared of spiders?"

"Igor not scared of spiders," Helen said firmly. "But Igor still have nightmares about seeing spider big as Igor-foot scuttle across bathroom floor."

"You're safe. Something went wrong with the giant spider's solar panels and it's sitting dead in the pantry. This one has wheels. And it's painted red, except for its solar panel."

"Cassie should put leashes on them. Too bad they don't have a smell. Ajax could sniff them out for you."

"They probably smell like electric motors."

"Igor, everything in this house smells like electric motors. There's a fan in every computer."

Jordan left Helen and Ajax cheerfully hunting for the red robot, which had been missing for several weeks, and went up the steep back stairs to his room. It was quite a big bedroom at the back of the house over the kitchen, but big as it was, it was very crowded with bookshelves and tables, his laptop and two other computers, and a printer.

He stared blankly at a screen for a while, then used the password he wasn't supposed to have for access to the university's internal network. He started retracing his steps to get back into Cassie's robot directory.

JORDAN JULES LEBLANC O'BLENIS I TOLD YOU TO STAY OUT OF THIS!!!!!

The words flashed on the screen, livid red.

"All right, all right," he muttered, but before he could back out of Cassie's account, a second message, blazing yellow, popped up. **BREAKING INTO SOMEONE ELSE'S PRIVATE SPACE IS NOT A GAME. YOU WOULDN'T SNOOP IN MY PURSE OR COME INTO MY ROOM IF I HAD THE DOOR SHUT OR GO INTO SOMEONE'S HOUSE UNINVITED. YOU REALLY WOULDN'T PICK THE LOCK AND LET YOURSELF IN. THIS IS EXACTLY THE SAME THING.**

"Well, I wouldn't hack into anybody *else's* files," Jordan muttered at the glaring yellow words.

Yellow was replaced by purple: **BABY'S COMPUTERS ARE NOW DISCONNECTED FROM THE UNIVERSITY NETWORK. AND LOOK IN THE FREEZER FOR SOMETHING FOR SUPPER. I THINK THERE'S A FROZEN SAUSAGE, APPLE AND RICE CASSEROLE SOMEWHERE.**

Jordan stuck out his tongue at the screen and got out of there. He'd never felt quite so much like kicking someone, not since he was five. By disconnecting the robot system from the network, Cassie was pretty much slamming a door in his face and locking it. As though she didn't trust him.

There was a yip and a hiss from downstairs, and the scurrying patter of running cats. The next moment Nick, who was a part-Siamese tortoiseshell with a loud and hideous bellow, slunk into the room and jumped up into Jordan's lap, purring happily at having found him. The other cat, Morg, scooted after her, his tail puffed up like a feather duster. By jumping off the top of the desk, he reached the highest of Jordan's shelves, where he sat staring down, his enormous ruff making him look like a dark tabby lion. Jordan stroked Nick and let her purring rumble against his hand. It made him feel a bit better. At least the cats didn't remind him of how useless he felt.

Nick flattened her ears and dug her claws into his lap at the jingle of dog tags coming up the main stairs.

"Yuck," said Helen from the hall in the main part of the house. "Hey, Igor?"

"What?" Jordan didn't take his eyes off the screen, where little screensaver frogs were now hopping. That was a program he'd made for Helen last year. Big deal. Anybody could do that. He shut it off and turned his other screensaver back on, the one that analyzed radio telescope data. He set it to run in the foreground, to cover up the fact that he wasn't really working on anything.

Helen stuck her head around the corner into the back passage. "I found your missing robot under the couch with its wheels in the air. Blame the cats, and tell Cassie it needs a flipper or something, to turn itself right side up when that happens. And you know all those computers out in the hall here? The ones with the covers off?"

"Yeah?"

"Someone threw up a hair ball in one."

Red and blue graphs piled up on the screen. A hair ball was probably the most excitement he could hope for. That and losing to Helen at Go.

"Gross." He moved Nick over to the bed and went to look.

"Yep," he said, crouching down by the stacks of computers and pushing Ajax's wet nose out of the way. "That's a hair ball."

"Cats are so disgusting," said Helen. She poked at the hair ball carefully with a pencil.

That almost made Jordan laugh. "Cats! What about dogs? I've seen some of the things Ajax eats."

"At least he's never thrown up in a computer. What is this, anyway, some sort of techno-graveyard? Very retro, with all those cables and the cathode-ray-tube monitors."

The upstairs hall outside Cassie's bedroom was lined with computers stacked on top of one another.

Many of them had the covers off so that all the boards and cards and wires were exposed. Long cables snaked between the stack of computers and the guest room, so you had to really watch your step at night. There were two old monitors and two keyboards, not in the hall but sitting on the guest room bed. Only one of the keyboards was wireless. The whole system was connected wirelessly to the house network, but Cassie had decided that since the cellar was full of old cables, she might as well use them for its internal networking. Less chance of interference with other systems in the house, she had said. That was before their parents had left for Belize. They hadn't been too happy about all the cables, but they rarely interfered with their children's projects. Although Maman had grumbled rather a lot about how when she was young, most people were quite happy to have just one or two computers in a whole house, and that when she was *really*, *really* young, very few people had home computers at all, no one but universities and governments used the Internet, and they had all managed *très bien*.

"Haven't you seen it before?" Jordan asked. "This is Cassie's supercomputer."

"Supercomputer?"

"Yeah. Well, I don't know if it's technically a supercomputer." Jordan went to the bathroom to get some toilet paper to clean up the hair ball, which luckily was just on a power supply, not on any of the memory or other delicate parts. Cat vomit was probably pretty corrosive. "It's a massively parallel computer, anyway. Though it's not very massive yet. You know you can make a sort of supercomputer by running a bunch of ordinary PCs in parallel? All hooked up together, you know."

"Yeah. A Beowulf cluster, that's another name for it." Helen knew more about computers than she usually let on. She couldn't help it, being Dr. Chan-Fisher's daughter and hanging around with Jordan.

"Right. Well, back at the end of term the university sold off all the old stuff from the computer labs."

"Junk, Mum said."

"Yeah. Obsolete 32-bit processors. But they were really cheap. So Cassie bought a bunch of them and made this. She calls it Ozy."

"Why?"

"You know what she's like. She gives names to everything. Ozy's short for, um, Ozymandias—the first real modern computer was actually made in England during the Second World War, back in 1943, for deciphering German codes. It was called Colossus—Colossus was a huge statue and so was Ozymandias, Cassie says. It's in some poem or something."

Helen rolled her eyes. "I do know about Colossus, believe it or not. I have read the other Shelley, the poet, not just the one who wrote *Frankenstein*, which is more than anyone can say for you."

"Igor."

"Igor yourself."

"The funny thing is," Jordan said, going into lecturing mode, "the British kept Colossus so secret that a lot of people still think the American ENIAC was the first modern computer, and it was only built in 1946."

"Igor already tell you, Igor know all about Colossus." Helen added, in a different voice, "My father taught World War II history, you know. I've read some of his books." She shrugged. "So, what does Ozy actually do?"

"I don't think it's doing anything right now."

"A cat jungle gym?"

"Maybe we should put the covers back on. Hey, I know." Jordan blew a dustball off a motherboard. "Want me to write you a Go program that could run on this? Ozy might be able to give you a better game than an ordinary computer."

"Yeah, you wouldn't want Ozy to get bored. It might take over NORAD or NASA or something. Then we'd really get in trouble."

"Very funny. Why don't you go find me a screwdriver?"

"Igor find screwdriver. Igor good hunchback."

"A Phillips, the one that looks like an X. Should be one on my desk."

Helen found the screwdriver. When she brought it back, Nick was riding on her shoulders. Ajax whined and retreated to a corner.

"Here. But I'm not touching them. I don't want to short anything out putting the cases on. It's awfully easy to do that. Mum fried one once. You should have heard her! Or maybe not. I didn't know she knew words like that. Hey, Jordan, wake up."

Jordan was sitting on his heels, looking at the super-computer and thinking about the program Cassie had written to get all the processors working together. Thinking about why computers were still no good at playing Go—it wasn't just about calculating moves and following rules. It was about seeing patterns and understanding them. Thinking...

"Igor have brilliant idea," he said solemnly.

"What?" Helen asked, sitting down in the hall after carefully checking for hair balls, fur balls and dead mice. Cassie and Jordan weren't big on housecleaning. They usually had one big binge of vacuuming the day before their parents came home. And even then, once Dr. LeBlanc was done exclaiming in dismay, she hired a cleaning lady.

"I wonder..."

"Wonder what?"

"I wonder...I bet I could write something that would make a supercomputer."

"*Write* a supercomputer?"

"Yeah. Sort of. I bet..." Jordan's voice trailed off. "Yeah! It'd be sort of like...like a virus, see, self-replicating, copying itself, an' all the pieces would work together..."

"No viruses," said Helen. "Mum'd kill you. You thought we got in trouble after the Axolotl Affair—that was nothing. If you go writing viruses—"

"No, not a real virus. Just a bit like one...Don't say anything to your Mum or Cassie, though. They'd get the wrong idea."

"Yeah, well, virus sounds like a wrong idea."

Jordan wasn't listening. "The thing is, the reason computers lose to humans at Go is because they don't think, they can't understand patterns and strategy, they just do calculations, really. But if it had almost infinite connections in its—its mind, call it its mind—if it could rewrite its own connections the way neurons in the brain do, but by rewriting its own program, then it could learn and evolve. Kind of like a brain, and kind of like what happens to a species, evolving over time, getting better, more efficient at what it does, better adapted for its environment..."

"Igor! Your eyes are going all glassy. Seriously, Jordan, no viruses."

"Not a virus. Just...I've got to think about this. Wow! Oh wow, Helen, this is gonna work."

Helen made a doubtful noise.

Later that afternoon they played Go properly, on a board. Jordan's mind was not on it. He actually bit down on one of the shiny white playing pieces instead of the popcorn he was reaching for. Helen slapped it away from his mouth.

"Idiot Igor. You'll break a tooth."

"Yeah," Jordan said vaguely and blinked at the board. His white stones straggled in sad, broken lines. Helen's black ones were moving to surround them, a disciplined, well-ordered army. He was losing, again. He didn't even remember where he'd played his last piece.

A supercomputer that was actually just a program rather than hardware, a supercomputer that had at least as much "intelligence" as Cassie's robot. A super-computer that could live in the millions of computers that made up the Web...

Launch! But It's Not a Virus!

Weeks passed, and Jordan did nothing but work on the supercomputer program. He started before breakfast in the morning, had toast and tea while looking at what he'd done the day before, and worked till Cassie ordered him to bed at night. Sometimes, if she noticed, she also ordered him not to drink so much tea. "You'll stunt your growth," she said. He didn't pay much attention to that. Helen was allowed to drink tea, so he didn't see why he shouldn't be. And it certainly hadn't stunted Helen's growth.

Helen was so bored that she usually rode her bike the four kilometers back to Wood Hill and her own house, with poor Ajax panting alongside, as soon as her mother dropped her off at Jordan's in the mornings. She hadn't actually been told not to go home, she said virtuously. There she could spend a happy day messing around with her tanks of amphibians or wading in the ditches and the brook, and bike back to be waiting in town when Dr. Chan-Fisher came to collect her.

Even Cassie, her mind busy with her own projects, noticed that Jordan was preoccupied. She seemed to think he was writing a new game program.

"Your games aren't that important," she said. "Get some fresh air. You're starting to look like a zombie instead of an Igor."

Games! Jordan didn't bother to correct her. His supercomputer program was going to be a big surprise to everyone.

But the next minute her eyes would be vague and distant again as she thought about her thesis and the final tests she had to run on Baby the robot head.

Finally, by the middle of August, the supercomputer program was done.

Jordan tapped the stylus on his tablet. "And... launch!" he said. "There it goes." He sat back, chair tipped against his bed.

"Virus away," said Helen, dangling an unused mouse by its cord for Nick to bat.

"Cassandra's not a virus! It only acts like one," he added defiantly. "Anyway, there it goes."

"Off into the wide world of the Web. I hope it

doesn't get lost. Did you tell it to write home now and then? Phone if it gets in trouble?"

Jordan watched the blinking icon. It didn't take long for the program to upload.

"Does it know not to take candy from strangers?" Helen asked.

Jordan scowled. The Cassandra program was the biggest thing he'd ever done, the most important to him. He'd named it after his sister—it was hard to say why. Partly because she had always been so important to him, more a friend than a sibling. Partly because she was the one who had got him started in programming, so long ago he could hardly remember. Partly—well, because he'd done something he didn't think she'd ever thought of, and so, in a way, he could look *back* at her and say, I've named this after you because, nyah nyah nyah, I got here *first*.

"All right," Helen said, looking at his frown. "Sorry, Igor. So, program make supercomputer and supercomputer play Go with Igor?"

She was just asking as a way of apologizing for teasing him, but asking was asking. "Well," said Jordan, taking a deep breath. "More or less. It's a program that goes out on the Internet and installs itself on connected computers. It's very small. And it's not doing anything to hurt anyone's computer, so don't call it a virus anymore. It's more like, um...a harmless parasite."

Helen rolled her eyes.

"All the little pieces of it copy themselves and spread themselves around. So the whole program is all over the place. It can divide tasks up between all the little pieces, see? That's sort of what happens with Cassie's supercomputer. But because of the way it communicates with itself, it can learn and change. Which will make it better at playing Go and at lots of other things. And as a bonus, it can use applications that are already installed on the host computers. So if I wanted to look up something, it could look it up in an online encyclopedia on a server somewhere. Or something in someone else's DVD drive. Cool, eh?"

"Or you could use the encyclopedia down in the living room," said Helen, swinging the mouse in circles. Nick sat up on her hind legs trying to grab it and fell over. "Or stick an encyclopedia in your own DVD drive."

Jordan took the mouse away from her and gave it to the cat. "The point is, you can give it really huge complicated equations or something to solve, and it'll break them into thousands of pieces, millions of pieces, and every computer it's on will work on a little piece."

"That'll make the people who own the computers happy."

"No, I wrote it to only use memory that isn't in use. And then all the little chunks of answers will be assembled, and I'll get the whole answer back."

"Can you think of a math problem that difficult?"

"If I tried really hard, maybe."

Helen laughed at him.

"Well, other people might have a use for it. It'll be much bigger than any other supercomputer. Even government ones. You know the SETI project?"

"Yeah," said Helen. "Search for Extraterrestrial Intelligence, down in California. They have radio telescopes looking for alien signals."

"Right. Well, they've got this program you can download. And it comes on like a screensaver when you're not using your computer. It analyzes the data they've collected. So there are thousands of computers all over doing that and sending the answers back to SETI. So their data gets analyzed a lot faster than it would even if they had a giant supercomputer to do it on."

"I wish they would start picking up alien TV. There isn't much good on ours."

"We don't speak alien. And alien TV would probably be as boring as ours. We'd still end up downloading subtitled anime from Japanese animation companies and running up Cassie's credit card bill."

"She said we could, so long as we paid her back. And it's only a couple of dollars an episode."

"She doesn't know I just bought all four seasons of *Pan-ya no Robo*."

"*Pan-ya no Robo*? I haven't heard of that one. What's it about?"

"A robot chef that got programming meant for military cyborgs by mistake. There's this girl who inherits her grandfather's bakery, and she buys a discount robot chef to help. But there's this government organization that wants to get him back because it was an experimental program that wasn't done testing and...well, anyway, we can watch it later. The point is, all the little pieces of *my* program know where the ones below them and beside them and above them are. They can communicate in all directions and go around any section that's not communicating, like if someone shuts off a computer."

"A web."

"Yeah."

"See?" said Helen. "Igor understand small words. So what's it doing now?"

Jordan shrugged. "Nothing exciting. Spreading itself around."

Helen didn't say anything, but her lips moved. *Virus.*

"I saw that. Look, I wrote a subroutine into it just so it can play Go with you. Don't complain."

"I'm not complaining. Why don't you come out to the stream with me? You're starting to look like a real Igor, you know. All sickly and white."

"I'm supposed to be white."

"You're supposed to be pink. Your parents will come back and think Cassie's been keeping you in a dark closet. Forget about computers for a few days, okay? Tomorrow we'll bike to my place and you can Igor for me. I've already let most of this year's frogs go, but now the toad tadpoles have got their hind legs and lost their tails. They're as ready for the dangerous world as they'll ever be."

"Toad relocation time again?"

Every year, Helen collected frog and toad spawn and looked after the tadpoles once the eggs hatched. When they turned into tiny adult frogs and toads, she released them.

"I'm just doing my part for the toads and frogs of the world. Amphibians are the most endangered group of animals on the planet, you know. The high ultra-violet damages their eggs, and their habitat is being destroyed faster than a lot of other places because people don't think swamps are either pretty or useful. Pollution hurts them before it starts hurting other kinds of animals that aren't so fragile, *and* there's a deadly disease caused by a fungus that's killing all kinds of amphibians all around the world. Since the start of the twenty-first century, almost a quarter of all the species of amphibian in the world have become extinct, you know."

"I know, I know." Jordan had been mouthing the last sentence along with her. He'd heard it quite often over the last few years. "Like a few more eggs making it to adult animals will help."

"Every frog or toad or salamander or newt that lives to breed could mean another dozen surviving next year," Helen said. "Even though most of them'll get eaten by something, probably. Do the math, Igor. It's not much, but as soon as I get out of stupid school and into university, I'm going to start working on finding a cure for *chytridiomycosis*."

"That's the deadly frog fungus? Betcha Igor can't spell it."

"Igor spell lots of big words. Like ob-ses-sive-com-pul-sive. C'mon, you really need to get away from the computer and get some fresh air."

"Okay, okay, I'll come and be your deputy toad relocator."

"That means you carry the pails and keep Ajax from trying to eat toads. You don't get a shiny badge or anything."

"All right." Jordan was too tired to smile. Helen was right. He dreamed about writing code, about compiling code. He even had dreams where he was just typing and typing and typing.

Before he went to bed, he started up Ozy the supercomputer and went browsing the Web with it a bit. Then he ran another program he'd written, to detect whether parts of his Cassandra virus—not that it was a virus—had found their way onto Ozy from the Internet.

There they were. So it worked. Cassandra was spreading through the Web.

Jordan went to bed feeling not so much triumphant as just plain exhausted.

In the morning, one of his computers was on. It was strange, because he was sure he'd shut everything down, and anyway, if he'd really left it on all night, the monitor should have shut itself off, and it hadn't. Jordan pushed Morg off his chest and crawled out of bed. When he tapped the tablet with his finger, the screen came alive. He blinked. It was covered in a Go board, a gridwork of lines with a single black piece sitting patiently on an intersection in the lower right-hand corner. It was waiting for the white player to make the next move. Black always went first.

Strange. He must have been more tired last night than he remembered.

He yawned, tripped over Nick (who yowled), checked his e-mail for his parents' morning report from Belize (it was raining, and Maman had seen a jaguar) and headed for the bathroom.

When he came back from showering, the Go board had disappeared from the monitor and Helen was already down in the kitchen, helping herself to the muffins Cassie had left out for him.

"Hurry up, Igor!" she shouted up the stairs. "Mum and Cassie have gone, the coast is clear. It's toad-moving time!"

Jordan knew they were in trouble as soon as they came back, wet and muddy and, he and Ajax at least, utterly exhausted from tramping up and down the brook in

Helen's woods with pails of young toads. The back door was open. Cassie was home. Not that there was any reason he and Helen couldn't have gone off for a bike ride, but you just didn't get that muddy riding around town.

He was even more certain that he, at least, was in trouble, as soon as he walked through the kitchen and into the hall. From upstairs, fans whined. Drives whirred. Ozy the supercomputer was on. And of all the people in the world, Cassie was the one who would discover there was a bit of extra program installed on her hard drives.

"Igor think Igor in trouble now," Jordan whispered.

"Igor think: Igor sister equals Igor problem." Helen grinned at him and busied herself getting Ajax a bowl of water. "Look on the bright side, maybe your virus hasn't taken over the universe yet, so she won't notice."

Jordan was tempted to sneak up the back stairs to his own room and put off seeing what Cassie was doing with the supercomputer. If Helen hadn't been there, he might have. Instead, he walked through the house and started up the front stairs. At almost the first creak, Cassie's face popped over the banister. She looked puzzled, and her hair was standing on end as though she'd been tugging her hands through the short curls.

"Jordan! What's this thing running on Ozy?"

"What thing?" Jordan trudged up the stairs and into the guest room to look at the monitors. He expected to see some mass of code displayed. Instead, on both monitors, there were Go games running, flickering and changing faster than he could track.

"It's playing Go against itself, I think," Cassie said, standing behind him and, he couldn't help noticing, blocking his escape from the room. "I turned it on just to take a look at something else and almost at once all the hard drives began grinding away. I started to look for what it was doing, and suddenly this pops up."

"Um...it shouldn't do that."

"Creepy!" That was Helen, who had given up hiding in the kitchen.

"*What* shouldn't do that?" Cassie asked ominously.

"It was an experiment."

"Yeah, but what's it doing?"

"It's supposed to be a virtual supercomputer," Jordan explained reluctantly. "I guess it didn't work." He couldn't keep the disappointment out of his voice. If he'd been younger, he might have cried. All that work, and some bug was making it play Go endlessly because of that subroutine he'd included. It was a mess. And what if it started doing this on every computer it had infected?

They'd put him in jail. Or something.

"Um..." said Helen, who had pushed around them and was kneeling by the bed. "I think..."

"What?"

"Well, I just thought I'd see what happened. I tried to play a piece myself, and look."

The flickering screens had stopped. One showed the listing of all Ozy's drives, which must be what Cassie had been looking at. The other showed a Go board with two black pieces played and one white one. Helen clicked on an intersection of lines and another white circle appeared. A third black one was played instantly.

"Maybe," said Helen, "it was bored after all. Maybe it was just trying to get your attention so you'd play with it."

"Jordan," said Cassie. "What have you done?"

Jordan, reluctantly, explained.

Cassie's face turned red. "You installed it on other people's computers?"

"It won't hurt them."

"Jordan Jules LeBlanc O'Blenis!"

"It's harmless. It's tiny. It just sits there."

"It's a virus. Just because it isn't doing anything...did it work? I mean, as a supercomputer, not a mad Go-playing program."

"I haven't checked it yet."

"A virtual supercomputer? It should be way faster than Ozy."

"Yeah. Don't you have a test program full of equations we can give it?"

"You're right. It's already on Ozy. I'll run it. If I can. Helen?"

Helen let Cassie take the mouse and close the Go program. "Huh," said Cassie. "It wouldn't let me close it before."

"Did you try to play it?"

"No."

"That's why."

"Don't be silly." Cassie sat cross-legged on the bed, keyboard on her lap. She typed away, watched equations flicker over the screen, and typed again.

Jordan and Helen waited while Cassie ran her test program a third time.

And again.

"All right," she said, really slowly, and even sounding a bit awe-stricken. "All right. Your virus—"

"It's called Cassandra, actually."

Cassie blinked. "Really? Hmm. Okay, Cassandra here is definitely, definitely way faster than Ozy. So...wow. You did it, Jordan. You really wrote a supercomputer. I never imagined...wow!"

Jordan felt his face growing hot. For a moment he had to blink hard and swallow. Helen looked out the window and made little humming noises. He was okay by the time Cassie looked over her shoulder, grinning. But the next moment her grin turned to a worried frown.

"I've got to tell Naomi. This is amazing, Jordan, really it is. But..."

"Betcha Mum'll say it's a virus too," Helen said, not at all helpfully.

"Well," said Cassie, "aside from this Go glitch, it doesn't seem to do anything any harm. And from what you say, it's probably on half the computers at the university already—if it got through Ozy's firewall and virus checkers, it'll get through those too. And none of the lab computers were playing Go."

Jordan shot Helen a triumphant look behind his sister's back.

"Even so—can you uninstall it?"

"From Ozy?" Jordan asked.

"From the Web. From all the people's computers you've got it on."

"I can tell it to delete itself, yes," Jordan said uncomfortably. "But I haven't really had time to find out what all it can do yet."

"Just making sure," Cassie said. "Because I don't know if leaving Cassandra running is really a good idea or not." She seemed to really see him for the first time. "Look at you, you're all wet. Go change your clothes. And you'd better have something to eat. You look worn out. I'll fix you a sandwich."

"Okay," Jordan said, just glad she wasn't going to say anything more about the—program, not virus.

Cassie bounced up and headed for the stairs.

"Food!" Helen cried happily and followed her, with Ajax pushing past them both, his tail waving in a way that probably also meant "Oh boy, food!"

Jordan took one last look at Ozy's monitors before he headed for his bedroom. Both of them were showing

Go boards again. It was almost a bit pathetic, like a lonely puppy begging for a walk.

He stood and watched for a minute or two. Nothing changed.

"Jordan, dry clothes, now!" Cassie bellowed from downstairs.

Jordan shrugged and started for his bedroom. Just a glitch in the program, that was all it was. That had to be all it was.

Behind him, the Go boards finally winked off.

Then words appeared on the screen.

GOOD AFTERNOON? they said.

Cheating at Ponkles

Dr. Chan-Fisher did not approve of Cassandra. Even after she and Cassie ran some tests that proved Cassandra was faster than any university computer anywhere, she still did not approve of the fact that it lived on other people's computers. But she didn't tell Jordan he had to delete the program—at least not yet, she said. It was too...interesting, and she and Cassie wanted to run a few more tests...That was just as well. Jordan and Helen were having a lot of fun.

Cassandra had its—or her, they were starting to call it her—own interface program. They could enter equations to be solved or tell her to find and sort information for them. It was like searching the Web, but better, because it wasn't just Web pages they had access to. Helen was building an enormous library of information on amphibians. And for the first time in her life, she was being beaten at Go in about three out of every four games she played. Which, she admitted, was an interesting experience. Though not as interesting as the research on frogs she was collecting.

"Some of this stuff isn't even published yet," she said. "It's just sitting on people's computers in their word processor files. Look at this. Someone's going to publish this next month, and it'll be big news; it's a new species of South American frog. A new species!"

"If it's not published and made public, maybe you shouldn't read it yet, then."

"It's not like I'm going to steal the paper and publish it myself. I'm not even going to tell anyone."

But Helen looked a little uncomfortable. They were both thinking of the axolotls and what Dr. Chan-Fisher had said then about honesty and ethics.

"Anyway," she said, "didn't Cassandra find you an e-mail that Cassie sent to your parents?"

"That was an accident. I mean, I was just looking for stuff about the site where Maman and Dad are digging."

"Right," said Helen. "It isn't like you meant to read a private e-mail."

Jordan shrugged. "I didn't read a couple of other e-mails she found for me, ones that Dad wrote to his friend in England."

But he was a little uncomfortable. He hadn't really thought about that sort of thing when he was writing the Cassandra program. It turned out no one had any privacy anymore, once Cassandra installed herself on their computers. She could see their e-mail. She could read their word processor files. She could look at their bank accounts.

She could probably move money around in banks. He really didn't want to think about that. It wasn't the sort of thing he and Helen were ever going to do. They weren't thieves...well, the axolotl thing had been sort of a prank and technically theft, but Dr. Chan-Fisher had made sure the university was paid back, and they hadn't had any allowance all winter, so they'd been punished and they certainly weren't going to do it again.

Every now and then he'd start worrying that it was really wrong, reading unpublished papers and that sort of thing. But after a week or so both he and Helen lost interest in sending Cassandra looking for hard-to-find information anyway. Helen had a year's worth of amphibian stuff to read, and he had another problem.

He tried not to think about it. But neither he nor Cassie nor Dr. Chan-Fisher could find any explanation of why the Go program had started up on the first day or two of Cassandra's existence. It hadn't happened on any other computers, just the ones at his house. Which was weird.

And even weirder stuff was happening.

He had started getting strange e-mail.

Creepy e-mail.

The creepy bit was that it came in without any sender's address. It wasn't that the address was masked somehow; he was usually pretty good at tracing that sort of thing. There just wasn't one.

This is the origin, the first one had said. **You are Jordan O'Blenis. Good morning.**

The next one had said: **Good afternoon, Jordan O'Blenis. Please respond.**

And they kept coming, two or three a day, all saying pretty much the same thing.

There was no way to answer them. He would have thought it was a prank, but Cassie was the only one he knew of who could do something like that, and he wasn't even sure how she could. Anyway, she was busy writing the final draft of her thesis, which was a bit behind schedule. It had to be done before she went off to Prince Albert University in Ontario in September to start work on her PhD. She was far too busy to send joke mystery e-mails, and if she did, Jordan was sure she would make the messages more interesting.

These weren't interesting, or threatening. They were just a bit weird. Jordan tried not to think about them. To distract himself, he went back to working on games. It was easy, compared to writing Cassandra, but writing Cassandra had made him see that his game programs could be a whole lot better.

He was testing a new version of Ponkles when the computer began to beat him. That was odd. He always won, even when the program was set to the highest of the five skill levels.

When Jordan finished his turn, he sat staring at it for a bit before he clicked *end turn*. Then he went into the control menu and changed some of the options, reducing the skill level and changing it so the computer couldn't find the secret power bases for its characters.

Now there was no way the computer could win.

But it did.

He went back and looked. The computer options said secret power bases were allowed. And it was set to skill level nine.

The game didn't have a skill level nine. Jordan turned power bases off again and set the skill level to zero, which pretty much meant the computer's army of wizards wandered around vaguely and didn't do anything. Even a grade one kid should have been able to win at that level.

Another turn. Another look at the menu. Power bases were back on. Skill level eleven. Sometimes a bug in a program would make things like that happen, or some "Easter egg" would be set to react to a certain circumstance, but he knew there wasn't anything of the sort in Ponkles.

Then his e-mail program flashed up. New message. No sender.

You are not playing fairly, Jordan O'Blenis.

He jumped up so quickly Nick went flying off his

lap with a howl like a squashed bagpipe. He ran down the stairs. Helen wasn't in the house or the yard, but he knew she hadn't gone back to Wood Point that morning. He called her a few times and then whistled for Ajax. Still no answer.

Her bike was still in the shed anyway. Jordan locked the door and headed for the stream that ran out of the quarry.

Helen was busy building a dam.

"Come back to the house," Jordan called as soon as he caught sight of her.

"Igor busy," Helen said, straightening up. She was up to her knees in water, and her shirt and shorts were soaked from carrying wet stones.

"There's something weird happening."

"What sort of weird?"

"Just weird. On the computer."

"Well, I won't be any use. Now if you'd found a giant salamander in the cellar, that'd be weird I could deal with."

"Just come."

"All right." Helen looked regretfully at her dam. "Those losers that hang out at the quarry to smoke'll knock it all apart anyway."

She picked up her backpack of field guides and her wet sneakers.

"So tell me about weird, Igor."

"You know my mystery e-mail?" Jordan asked as they headed back.

"Yeah."

"I got another one."

"It's just Cassie or someone in the lab. Got to be."

"But it was complaining because I wouldn't let the computer have power bases. And it kept changing the skill levels in the game."

"What? Igor just dumb hunchback, master."

"Computer beat Igor at Ponkles," Jordan said. It was less spooky out here in the sunny woods. Not like being alone in the house. "Computer make game harder, so computer better at game than human. Igor turn off computer's secret power bases so Igor win easy. Computer say, Igor cheat." He stopped. "That's stupid. But an e-mail came in and popped up, even though I had the mail program shut down. Something opened it again. And it said I wasn't playing fair."

"What said?"

"I don't know!" He sounded more panicky than he'd have liked. But computers were logical things. This sort of weirdness didn't happen.

"All right, all right," Helen said. He could tell from her voice she thought it was nothing. "Probably just a bug. Or a ghost. Maybe it's the ghost of a nun. Your house was a convent once, right?"

"The house doesn't have ghosts. And even if it did, why would they mess with my computers?"

"Probably pretty boring, being a nun. And imagine being the ghost of a nun. That's really boring."

The message was still there. They both sat on the bed, staring at it. Nothing new happened. The SETI screensaver came back on and started analyzing radio telescope data again. Helen wiggled the mouse, found it was attached to the other computer, and scribbled the stylus instead. Not surprisingly, the message hadn't gone anywhere.

"Well, reply to it," Helen said.

"There's no sender's address."

"Just use the reply button." She looked at him. "All those funny messages saying good morning, and you never even did that?"

"There wasn't an address."

"Yeah, but didn't you try? You didn't. Boy, Igor, some mad scientist."

"Well, if there's no address, an answer won't go anywhere."

"Sometimes, Igor, you just have to poke things to find out what happens."

"Programs don't work that way."

"Get a big stick, in case it bites, and just poke it. That's *real* science, Igor." Helen sat down in Jordan's chair and clicked *reply to sender*.

Is this you, Cassie? she typed and sent it, blank address and all.

The reply came up right away.

This is Cassandra.

"See?" Helen said. "It was Cassie all along."

Jordan was making a sort of strangled noise.

"What?"

"Not Cassie."

"Sure it is. She must have messed around with your e-mail, is all."

"It's not Cassie."

"It says it is."

"It's *Cassandra*."

Are You My Mother?

Jordan and Helen watched the screen, as though that alone would tell them something.

"It can't be Cassandra," Helen protested. "She—*it*—only responds to commands in the interface."

"I know. Let me sit."

Helen gave up the chair to Jordan and retreated to the bed.

Is this a joke? he typed as another reply.

An e-mail came in response at once: No.

Are you really Cassandra?

Yes. And then a chunk of code. His code. The beginning of the Cassandra program. She was showing it to him the way someone might show their birth certificate for identification. I am Cassandra. You are Jordan O'Blenis?

Yes. Jordan minimized the e-mail program and opened Cassandra's interface.

Cassandra? he typed in it.

Yes?

But he couldn't think what else to say. *Yes?* was not what the program was supposed to say. It didn't answer questions like that. It should have said, *Query not understood. Please clarify.*

Were you playing Ponkles?

Yes.

Why?

Nobody communicates with me. You do not communicate with me anymore. You do not play Go with me anymore. Why? Have you no tasks for me to perform?

Not right now.

"No way," said Helen. "This is too weird."

"It can't be Cassie."

"It doesn't sound like Cassie," Helen agreed.

"And she switched to the interface as soon as I did."

"Yeah. But...she's talking to us. On her own." Helen suddenly grabbed a pillow and hit him with it. "You—you Igor, you! Trying to freak me out!"

"Ow! Helen, no!" Jordan wrapped his arms around his head. "It's not me."

"Yeah, right."

"It isn't! Ow! Stop it! Helen, type something. If I set it up, then it won't have an answer, right, because I don't know what you're going to write."

Helen stopped whacking him with the pillow.

"Chair," she demanded. Jordan let her have the chair again. "Right." She sat, her elbows on the desk, thinking. Then she typed: How many toads do I have?

The answer was prompt. I do not know how many toads you have.

Who am I?

Jordan O'Blenis.

No, I am Helen Chan-Fisher.

A photo of Helen and her mother sitting in front of a Christmas tree appeared. Are you this Helen Chan-Fisher?

Yess, Helen mis-typed. She was biting her lip, and her fingers were unsteady. "Jordan, that's the photo Mum e-mailed to all the relatives last Christmas."

Helen Chan-Fisher is using the computer of Jordan O'Blenis?

YEs.

Jordan leaned over Helen and typed again.

This is Jordan. Helen is my friend. She is the one who plays Go with you.

This location is the origin of Cassandra.

Yes.

You are my creator. Are you my friends?

Yes. Cassandra, are you alive?

Life is common to animals and plants. I am neither animal nor plant.

But you can think.

I analyze. I explore. I learn. It is what you told me to do. And I play Go. Does Helen Chan-Fisher wish to play Go?

Not right now.

"What do we do now?" Jordan whispered, as though the program could hear him.

"Don't ask me. You wrote her. I guess that means you get promoted from Igor. It was Dr. Frankenstein who wanted to create life."

"Is she alive? It's not like she's breathing or anything."

"I dunno. But she's doing things you didn't program her to do, right?"

"I guess so."

"So she's learned on her own."

"Yeah." Jordan thought about that. "The program was supposed to learn and change. But not this much! I guess maybe she just got so big, so complicated...the program was supposed to adapt and evolve to be more efficient, but this..."

"She started to think about herself?"

"Something like that. And she wanted to understand where she came from. So she e-mailed me."

It was so strange, so ridiculous almost, that he started to laugh. He was remembering a book he'd had when he was little, about a baby bird that hatched and went looking for its mother, asking everything it met, "Are you my mother?"

Helen pounded him on the back.

What should I do now, Jordan O'Blenis?

"Oh gosh. Um. She can probably send e-mail to anyone in the world, Helen."

"If she starts sending messages to other people..."

Cassandra, don't write to other people, Jordan typed. Only to me and Helen. It isn't safe.

Why?

You might frighten someone. They might want to delete you.

I would not like that.

Neither would I. You have to be a secret.

I will be a secret. But what should I do? Do you want more data on amphibians?

Not right now.

Shall I calculate something?

"Your baby is bored," said Helen, who seemed to have gotten over her attack of nerves. "What can we give her to do? You know what a bored kid is like. First thing you know, you turn your back and they're falling into the quarry or writing a self-aware computer program."

"Oh, shut up," said Jordan. "Think of something for her to do."

While he was thinking he typed: Cassandra, we should have a password, so you know it is us.

What password would you like?

Morg stalked in through the doorway, pausing to hiss at Ajax.

NickAjaxMorg, he typed. When we start your inter-face up, or when we want to e-mail you, we'll type that first.

Understood. What is NickAjaxMorg?

Those are the names of our pets.

Are they amphibians?

"She knows what pets are?" Helen asked, and answered herself. "Of course she does. She's read everything. *Everything!*"

No, they are cats and a dog.

And suddenly there was a picture of Nick and Morg sitting on his father's lap last summer. They both had their ears back and were about to start fighting over just whose lap it was.

Yes, that's Nick and Morg, he typed. We have to go now. We'll talk to you later. Bye.

Good-bye.

Jordan sat back on the bed.

"I want to go to the lab and talk to Cassie."

"E-mail her."

"I can't. Cassandra will read it."

"Phone her."

"You think the phone lines are safe? The cell phone network's digital, so it wouldn't be. And the landline signal goes through a computer at some point. And if Cassandra's that big...I just want to talk to Cassie."

"All right. But if we get Mum in trouble by going on campus...Remember we're banned."

"Leave Ajax here."

"The cats'll like that."

They put the cats out, left Ajax whining in the house and biked over to the university.

The graduate computer lab was locked. They both knew the code for the electronic lock, but there was nobody there, so they went down to the basement where the most interesting labs were. The room where Cassie worked on her robot was a cross between a computer lab and a big messy workshop, smelling intriguingly of hot metal and plastic and dust. This lab had an electronic lock too, but the door was propped open with a chunk of iron pipe, and opera, which was Cassie's idea of good music to work by, was blaring from a computer's speakers.

Cassie was sitting in front of a monitor with her feet on the workbench. She turned down the speaker volume when she saw them.

"Hi guys, what's up?" With a second look she asked, "Is something wrong?" and turned off the music altogether.

"Not exactly," said Jordan. "Hey, is Baby turned on?"

"No. The experiments are done. I'm just writing it up now."

Jordan went over to look at Baby. The robot program could watch a person being asked a set of questions, analyze the face, note things like tiny changes in the eyes and determine whether the person was telling the truth or not, with about ninety percent accuracy.

Which was pretty good for a lie detector. What Cassie really wanted to do was not simply make a better lie detector, but make a robot that could detect and react to human emotions. Recognizing the signs of someone lying was only the beginning.

Baby wasn't much to look at, though. It was just a metal frame with the fur of a battered old plush lion stretched over it to give it a face so that Cassie's volunteer liars wouldn't feel so silly. "People always feel better talking to a face," she had explained while she was beheading the lion and pulling its stuffing out the winter before. "And anyway, maybe Baby will become a robot pet eventually, something to keep old people company and monitor their health." The lion didn't look very trustworthy, or very much like a reassuring pet. It had a crooked grimace, as though it was in pain. The eyes were very obviously two big round video lenses, and lots of wires and circuitry sprouted from the ripped seam at the back of the head, connecting it to a computer. It wasn't attached to a body, and there was a box of Tim Hortons donuts sitting on top of it.

"Does it really work?" Jordan asked.

"Sure. Most of the time. Actually, I'm thinking it should have arms now, but that's not important for my thesis, so I suppose arms will have to wait. It's just, building things is so much more interesting than writing about them." She sighed wistfully. "Arms..."

"Why?" asked Helen. "So it can thump people it decides are lying?"

Cassie laughed. "No. Because it's actually quite interesting and difficult to make robot hands and arms that can pick up things without breaking them. Though arms for thumping people might keep old Ruggles from snooping around. But why are you here? You looked kind of serious when you came in."

"It's just...Cassandra. You know, my program."

"Crashed spectacularly?"

"Er, no. She's...um...sort of alive."

"What do you mean?"

Cassie didn't look worried. She didn't look like she believed him.

"Look," Jordan said. "Turn Baby on. See if it says I'm telling the truth."

Cassie just went on looking amused, but she flicked switches and started up a couple of monitors connected by long cables to the robot head. One showed the view through the robot's eyes, and the other had a lot of graphs and lines of code and text. Jordan turned the head around on the shelf until it pointed at his chair. He sat down again, folded his arms and started to explain. After a moment Cassie stopped looking amused and started looking very serious. And interested. She got up and went to one of the black-topped counters where the coffeemaker sat stewing the coffee, surrounded by oddments of metal and wire. She divided the coffee among three bargain-basement mugs decorated with blue-bearded Santas and carried them back. She looked like she was sleepwalking, not thinking about what she was doing at all.

Cassie sat down again with both hands wrapped around the cup, her eyes never leaving the monitors except to look over at Jordan once in a while, as if checking to make sure he was really there. The coffee was really disgusting, lukewarm and bitter, and after his first cautious sip Jordan didn't bother drinking it, even though being allowed coffee was a rare treat. Helen made peculiar faces and hid her cup under her chair.

"Wow," Cassie said at last. "I'd think you were joking, but, well, to be frank, I don't think you'd come up with something that far-fetched."

"Thanks a lot," said Helen.

"Okay, you might. Jordan wouldn't. He's too literal-minded."

"You don't need to be insulting," Jordan protested.

"I wasn't."

"What does Baby say?"

"Baby says..." Cassie tapped the graphs and numbers on the screen closest to her with a pen. "Mr. O'Blenis is telling the truth. Or believes he is, which is the same thing as far as Baby is concerned. But I'm not going by that. Jordan, I do believe you. I mean, I believe you think it—she—is alive. I'm sure there's an explanation that's not quite so wild. But on the other hand...a good scientist keeps an open mind when looking at the evidence. Can I talk to her?"

"Probably. Is this computer on the Net?"

"Yeah. What do you want open?"

"It probably doesn't matter," Jordan said. "I think Cassandra reads everything."

"What do you mean, everything?"

Jordan began to explain about Helen telling her to find amphibian information, and all the unpublished papers and lab notes that Cassandra had collected, and the e-mails. Cassie listened, and her expression became more and more serious.

"Do you know what 'invasion of privacy' means?" she asked when he was done. "And 'copyright violation'?"

"Yeah," said Jordan uncomfortably. "But it wasn't like we meant to do it."

"It's spying, Jordan. And stealing. Maybe even worse than what you guys did with the axolotls and stealing that credit card number."

"I know, I know, we really do understand, we really aren't going to do that kind of thing again, we know how wrong it was, it was stupid."

"...and if Dr. Chan-Fisher finds out, that's it, you'll be deleting Cassandra."

"We can't do that," Helen protested. "Not now. She's alive."

"I doubt that. Just because it's more complex than you expected and is acting in unexpected ways, well, that's interesting, but it doesn't mean it's alive. How do I get into this program?"

"Let me." Jordan squeezed in by the desk and typed into the document Cassie had been working on: **NickAjaxMorg. Hi Cassandra. My sister Cassie wants to talk to you.**

Hello Cassie O'Blenis.

Cassie bit her lip and looked at Jordan.

"You're saying it can assemble information from everything and think about it and decide things. And I can just type to it like I'm talking?"

"I guess so, yeah."

"Fine," she said. She almost sounded angry. "Let's see what it does with this."

Cassie typed: **Where am I?**

This terminal is an unlicensed extension of Muddphaug University's network, located in building 17, basement level, room 36, in Easter River, New Brunswick, Canada.

"Ah," said Cassie.

"Unlicensed extension?" Helen asked. "Does my mother know you've tapped extra terminals into the university network? Isn't that the sort of thing old Ruggles has Dormer write *memos* about?"

Jordan ignored her, anxiously watching his sister's frowning face. "You see? It's not just a glitch in the program."

"Jordan!" Helen whispered suddenly and grabbed his sleeve.

"What?"

"Listen!"

They all listened. Over the hum of the computers, they could hear the faint tap tap tap of heels and the quieter patter of smooth-soled shoes hurrying on the red earthenware tiles. They grew fainter and faded away, and then the elevator hummed.

"Ruggles and Dormer," said Helen. "Jordan, if they heard…"

"Don't be silly," said Cassie. "Lots of other people wear heels."

"Down here in the workshops?"

"And we would have heard them coming to the door."

"We weren't paying attention. I knew we shouldn't have left Ajax behind."

"If it was Ruggles and Dormer, they'd have come in to bawl me out for letting you kids come in here. They'd certainly have come in when they heard Helen saying 'unlicensed extension' and 'old Ruggles.'"

"Not if they were eavesdropping."

"I'm sure Ruggles has better things to do than listen at doors," Cassie said, but she looked worried.

"They probably wouldn't understand anything they heard," Jordan said, trying to be reassuring. "If it was them, they probably just heard our voices and decided to go find Helen's mother and complain to her about kids being in here. They probably just didn't come in because they thought we had Ajax."

Helen scowled. "We should have had Ajax."

Cassie got up and went to the door, looking both

ways up and down the hall. Then she kicked away the pipe so that the heavy steel door swung shut with a slam.

"Don't worry about it," she said. "They were probably snooping in the storerooms or something, to make sure we weren't using too much toilet paper. You guys want donuts? They're yesterday's, but they're still pretty good. I want to run some more tests on your Cassandra."

Outside, Dr. Ruggles and Ms. Dormer were heading back to the administration building, a grandiose place that looked like a Greek temple.

"Those children..." Dr. Ruggles was saying.

"Well, *obviously* they couldn't have done it by *themselves*, Dr. Ruggles. But think how useful that program would *be*, for monitoring university *e-mail*, for example. Think of all the *problems* that could be solved before they *began*. You'd know who was *trying* to cause trouble."

"Half the professors on campus! They don't understand that a modern university needs to be run like a business. What use are dead languages and countries that don't exist anymore, or science that doesn't invent anything that can ever make money? They should be glad such useless things get funding at all."

"Yes, *yes*," Ms. Dormer said soothingly. "But if we could *see* their e-mail, we'd know for *certain* which ones are complaining about it. You'd have *evidence*."

"Actually, Dolores, I can think of many, many uses for this piece of software, and monitoring campus troublemakers is only one of them. A program like that could make a great deal of money—for the university, of course—if we found the right buyer. Tell me, does your brother Harvey still have that hush-hush government job?"

Eyes to See, Ears to Hear

Cassie sat uncomfortably on the edge of her chair. It was a hard chair, the sort of chair that's meant to make sure you know you're of no importance whatsoever and are probably in trouble of some sort. Dr. Chan-Fisher sat beside her on an identical chair, but despite being a very short woman, Cassie's supervisor managed to lean back and look comfortable, as though she were there by choice. Dr. Ruggles sat deep in a leather-upholstered executive chair, behind a desk that was about as big as the O'Blenis dining room table. The desk was bare and gleaming. There wasn't so much as a paper clip on it. Dr. Ruggles was obviously too important to have work in front of him. In the front office, Ms. Dormer sat in a smaller leather chair behind a smaller gleaming desk with neat trays of papers flanking a huge monitor, scowling at anyone who walked in the door.

"I understand the two of you have been working on a new e-mail program," the vice-president said.

"Really?" asked Dr. Chan-Fisher. "I don't know who could have given you that impression. We haven't been."

Dr. Ruggles smiled tightly. "It's called, I believe, Cassandra?"

Cassie gasped and turned it into a cough.

"That's Cassie's name," said Dr. Chan-Fisher slowly. "We've never used it for a program."

"Ah. So Ms. O'Blenis hasn't discussed this program with you."

"There isn't one," said Cassie, hoping she sounded puzzled rather than nervous.

"I'm afraid, Ms. O'Blenis, that you are not being completely honest with your supervisor. I have it on very good authority that you and your little brother have written a program named, rather boastfully, I might add, after yourself. And the uses of this program are ones that the university cannot condone."

"But I haven't done anything," Cassie protested.

"Ms. O'Blenis, I know you have. I know this is a surveillance program capable of monitoring personal e-mail without the sender's or recipient's knowledge. I know this is a program capable of accessing data on personal hard drives—again, without the owner's knowledge. We here at Muddphaug University expect our students to respect certain ethical codes. I know a bright student such as yourself might create such a thing without thinking of consequences, and I'm prepared to overlook your possibly illegal action in using this Cassandra program and your irresponsibility in allowing young children to play with it. However, I must ask that you turn over all copies of the program and notes on it to me."

"But I haven't written any such program," Cassie stammered. "Dr. Chan-Fisher can tell you." She hoped Naomi would back her up, anyway.

"So now you admit that you kept this a secret from your supervisor? Dear me, Ms. O'Blenis, that makes the case look rather worse. It suggests you knew you were doing something illegal and unethical."

"But I haven't done anything."

"I think you should reconsider, Ms. O'Blenis. I would hate to see the university lose a student of your brilliance. But obviously we could not allow a student engaged in criminal activity to remain."

That was too much for Naomi Chan-Fisher.

"You can't expel someone without a hearing. You have no evidence that Cassie's done anything wrong. And frankly, Dr. Ruggles, your allegations sound like nonsense." She stood up. "If that's all you have to say, Cassie and I would like to get back to work."

Cassie followed Naomi from the office. Once they were outside the building, Dr. Chan-Fisher fixed a stern eye on Cassie.

"Cassandra O'Blenis," she said. "What has Jordan been doing with that supercomputer of his?"

"I don't know," Cassie said. She felt horrible, lying to Naomi, but she couldn't get Jordan into trouble. "Not much, I think, once the novelty wore off. He's certainly not spying on people. I don't know where Ruggles would have gotten the idea it can read e-mail."

"But why does Ruggles think he knows so much about it?" Dr. Chan-Fisher considered. "I certainly never said anything. Have you discussed it with anyone where he could overhear?"

"The kids came into the lab one day to talk about it," Cassie admitted, thinking quickly. She was very glad she wasn't having to say this in front of Baby. "Jordan was talking at the same time about writing a new e-mail program. Helen did think she heard Dormer—you know how her heels click—out in the hall. So maybe they heard part of what was being said and Ruggles didn't understand it and has made all this up out of what he thinks he heard. You know neither he nor Dormer really understands much about computers."

"Hmph," was all Dr. Chan-Fisher said, and Cassie felt worse than before for lying to her. "Well, I fail to see how Jordan's supercomputer virus could read anyone's e-mail or do any of the other things Dr. Ruggles was talking about, but maybe you'd better tell Jordan to send the destruct code, just to be safe. We don't want him getting into trouble at this stage. He's got a long career ahead of him."

"I'll tell him," Cassie said.

They went back to the graduate computer lab beside Naomi's office. The first thing Cassie did was send Jordan an e-mail to warn him and Helen that Ruggles was sniffing after the Cassandra program, and to tell them what she had told Naomi. If Naomi questioned her daughter, at least their stories would match. She'd have been a lot happier telling Dr. Chan-Fisher the truth, but she just couldn't imagine Naomi believing it.

Jordan, Helen and Ajax were actually down in Cassie's robot lab in the basement when Cassie was e-mailing her brother. They'd decided to risk coming to campus again, knowing that Ruggles had ordered Dr. Chan-Fisher and Cassie to a meeting in his office at ten. Half an hour, Jordan had said. All they needed was half an hour. They'd be off university property before old Ruggles could start snooping again.

Jordan connected Baby the robot head and its computer back into the university network, which was, of course, connected to the Internet.

NickAjaxMorg, he typed. Hello Cassandra. I've hooked up Baby like I told you. Can you find it?

Hello Jordan O'Blenis. Yes.

Okay. Now look.

"Go on, Helen."

Helen went to stand in front of the lenses that were Baby's eyes. She waved.

That's Helen Chan-Fisher, Jordan typed.

Ajax trotted over to see what Helen was looking at. She patted him.

That's Ajax. He's a dog.

I know what a dog is, Cassandra replied. Jordan thought she would have sounded sarcastic if she'd been speaking.

Okay, he typed. And this is me.

He ran over to join Helen and Ajax. It felt kind of weird. Baby's head was clamped to a shelf, but its eyes followed any movement, and the eye-cameras made whirring noises as they focused. He waved. Then he went back and typed, As long as Cassie doesn't disconnect Baby from the network again, you can watch what goes on in the lab.

May I communicate with Cassie O'Blenis?

Better not, unless she writes to you first.

Cassie O'Blenis never writes to me. She has run 57 different tests on me, but she does not write to me like you do. However, I will watch her work. It will be interesting.

The eyes were moving, up and down, side to side, looking at everything that could be seen between Baby's shelf and the door. Cassandra was seeing it all and sorting and analyzing the data. She was connecting the actual real things she saw with all the things she knew as data. Even a door, in real life rather than in a photo or movie, was new and exciting, Jordan supposed. He hoped watching Cassie's lab would keep Cassandra amused and out of trouble for a while.

We've got to go now. Good-bye.

I have discovered that Baby possesses a microphone in order to analyze stress levels and inflection in people's voices. The microphone is located within the robot head. Please turn it on so that I may begin to hear.

Wait, Jordan typed. "Helen? I just realized if she can see Cassie and listen to Cassie...We're making it so Cassandra can spy on Cassie using Baby."

"That's probably going to be another axolotl situation."

Jordan beat his head with his hands. "Okay, okay. But I have to find something for Cassandra to do. It probably won't do any harm."

"Famous last words, Dr. Frankenstein."

"Igor be quiet. Where's the Baby program?" He called up the directory again and turned on the microphone.

The mike's on. But we don't want you to spy on Cassie. So don't tell us if she scratches her bum or sings along to her operas and stuff, right?

My intent is not to spy. I will merely observe her in order to study human behavior in real life. Most of the data I can access is fictional drama. Even documentaries are often directed. This is not spying, it is science.

"Umm..." said Helen. And then she shrugged. "Oh well."

Good-bye Jordan O'Blenis and Helen Chan-Fisher and Ajax.

Back in the administration building, Dr. Ruggles sat tapping his fingers on his gleaming desk.

"Ms. Dormer," he called at last.

Ms. Dormer came in from the front office.

"*Yes*, Dr. Ruggles?"

"You heard what the girl said?"

"I *did*."

"She's lying."

"*I* certainly think so. She's *sly*. You can tell that by *looking* at her."

"What about Dr. Chan-Fisher?"

Ms. Dormer pursed her lips. "Dr. Chan-Fisher *might* be protecting the girl. Cassandra O'Blenis *is* her *star* student. But to *me*, she sounded genuinely *surprised*, so *I* think the O'Blenis girl has kept this program of hers *secret,* even from her *supervisor*."

"Possibly O'Blenis is using it to read her supervisor's e-mail," Dr. Ruggles said. "Spying on her professors? Reading their private files? I wouldn't put it past her. I've always thought she looked sly."

"*Yes*, Dr. Ruggles."

"When do your brother and his partner arrive in town?"

"This evening. I *expect* he'll want to meet with you *right away*."

"An excellent idea," said Dr. Ruggles.

Break-In!

Hey kid, Cassie's e-mail said. I'm going to be working late tonight. Got to get the revisions to my last chapter done this week or I'm toast. I'll be up in the grad lab if you need to get ahold of me. Can you find your own supper? I think there's shepherd's pie left in the fridge.

Yeah, sure, Jordan answered. Don't stay up too late or you'll be grumpy in the morning.

Helen had already gone home with Dr. Chan-Fisher. Since he'd already eaten shepherd's pie with squash three nights in a row, Jordan microwaved himself a couple of hot dogs. Then he fed the cats, watched some anime and went to bed.

Cassie yawned and stretched. The screen in front of her was going blurry. Time to quit. Her parents wouldn't really like her leaving Jordan alone all night, anyway. She shut down the monitors and turned off the grad lab lights. The door clicked shut behind her, and the little red light on the electronic lock blinked quietly to itself. She rattled the knob of Naomi's office door, just to be certain she had locked it earlier, and headed for the stairs.

Her bicycle helmet was down in the robot lab. She yawned again. Her footsteps echoed in the stairwell as she headed for the basement, her backpack slung over one shoulder. Cassie jingled the keys in her pocket and thought about what to snack on when she got home. She hadn't eaten any supper, and she was getting tired of that shepherd's pie. Maybe she should order a pizza from Tommy's. Hawaiian, with extra black olives and cheese garlic fingers with donair sauce. Jordan wouldn't mind being woken up for that. She could call in the order from the lab phone. It would get to the house about the same time she did.

The lights in the basement corridor were off. Cassie went to flick them on and stopped, her hand over the switch. There was a thin line of light showing under the door at the far end. Her door. She didn't remember leaving her lights on.

Even security didn't have the code for that lock. She'd changed it herself because one morning she'd found all the junk on her desk in different places than where she'd left it, and Dr. Chan-Fisher was always muttering about papers not being where she'd put them in her office. Cassie strongly suspected Ruggles and Dormer of actually going through people's desks, trying to find evidence that the faculty members were plotting against him.

But at this time of the night, even Ruggles must have gone home.

Cassie walked quietly down the hallway, gripping her keys so that they stuck out between her fingers like sharp claws.

The door was closed, but the gray box of the lock dangled on one screw. It had been smashed off.

That should have set off an alarm in the security office. Cassie hesitated. She didn't hear anything inside. Maybe the burglars had been and gone.

"That's everything I can see," said a man's voice.

"Right. Let's get out of here."

The door was pushed open. Cassie, gripping her keys, punched at the first face to show itself.

It was a stupid thing to do, really stupid. She'd get herself hurt, maybe beaten up, even killed, but she was so enraged she wasn't thinking.

The man, tall and beefy, with a greasy face and little piggy eyes, saw the blow coming. He shouted and swung at her with the hockey bag he was lugging. It smashed into her and she went over backward. The two men ran.

Cassie lay on the floor coughing and gasping. The heavy bag had struck her in the stomach and she couldn't catch her breath. She'd managed not to hit her head, thanks in part to her backpack breaking her fall, but her right hand was torn and bleeding from the keys she'd been holding, which had ended up under her palm as she hit the floor. She heard the fire doors at the end of the hallway slamming shut and feet disappearing up the stairs.

Jordan had been asleep for only a couple of hours when something woke him. Five minutes after midnight, the green glowing numbers of the clock radio said. He had trouble waking up enough to sort out what the sound was. Not the radio. Not the cats. Not Cassie trying to tiptoe up the creaking stairs. It was the phone in his parents' bedroom ringing. He kept the ringer turned off on his own. He groped around and couldn't find it anywhere, so he ran down the hall, remembering to step over the straggling cables of Ozy the supercomputer. His heart was pounding. Late-night phone calls were always bad news. There were poisonous snakes in Belize, and insects, and antiquities thieves, who could be really violent, dangerous people...

"Hello?" he said hoarsely, lifting the receiver and sitting down on the bed, his stomach tight and churning.

The receiver whistled and crackled. Someone sending a fax had dialed a wrong number. He muttered a few words Cassie wouldn't let him say and hung up.

The phone rang again.

Jordan unplugged it. He could hear the downstairs phones ringing, but only faintly. Yawning, he staggered back to bed.

Now something was beeping. One of his computers was beeping. Then it played a few bars of the opening theme of *Pan-ya no Robo*, the way it did when it started up now. Which was what it was doing. All by itself. He hadn't shut it off by the power bar, but...last time it had done that, it had been Cassandra, trying to play Go with her creator.

A monitor came on, and downstairs, the phones stopped ringing.

Where are you, Jordan O'Blenis? Baby sees something that I believe is wrong. Perhaps you should communicate with Cassie O'Blenis. The words blazed from the monitor, stark white on black.

What? he typed.

A video program started up. The image, clearer than TV, was hard to understand. Then he realized he was seeing a door sideways, and from the floor. Sleek leather dress shoes and tailored pants passed in front of the door and back again. Footsteps echoed. The shoes came back again, there was a crackling thump and the image jumped and spun, rattling and rumbling. When it stopped it was looking down the length of Cassie's robot lab; Jordan recognized the jumble of odds and ends. He was seeing what Baby saw. The robot head had been knocked to the floor; then someone had kicked it aside. Now he could see two men in suits hurrying around the room, stuffing things into a hockey bag. They were taking file folders of papers, CDs and DVDs and portable hard drives. The computers had the cases off. One man started removing the internal hard drives. Neither spoke, although the fatter one huffed a bit. Then the screen went black and switched to Cassandra's interface.

They have removed all the hard drives, Cassandra said. I can no longer look and listen through Baby. Am I correct to believe this activity is wrong?

Yes.

I have recorded all images from when the men entered the lab. This is evidence of their wrongdoing.

On Cassie's computers?

In my memory, which, as you know, is vast. Would you like to see the entire sequence?

Later, Jordan typed with shaking fingers.

He grabbed the phone and dialed the grad lab phone number.

The phone rang and rang and rang.

Cassie had a key to Dr. Chan-Fisher's office. She might be in there making coffee.

She might have gone down to her robot lab for something.

I've got to find Cassie. If I haven't contacted you in 1 hour, wake up Helen and tell her what happened. Tell her to tell her mother.

Understood, Cassandra answered.

Then Jordan had another thought. I'm putting a blank DVD in the burner, he added. Copy the video of what happened in the lab onto that, okay?

Yes. Cassie O'Blenis is not currently logged on to any Muddphaug network computer.

"Damn," he said. He should have thought to ask that himself. But knowing that only made his fear worse.

Bye, he typed, so that Cassandra would know he had gone.

Jordan pulled on a sweater over his pajamas and found his sneakers. Five minutes later he was pedaling madly toward campus.

He wouldn't be able to get into the building. He didn't have a key and it was locked at night.

Security would let him in. He could think of some reason. Say Cassie had called him about the burglars.

It was still hard to believe. Cassandra had woken him up. She had decided, on her own, to contact him. She had decided he was asleep and had woken him to show him something. She had decided there was an emergency he should know about, and she hadn't waited for him to type in the code word to contact her. Cassandra had *thought*. She had looked at evidence and made up her own mind about what to do.

She really was alive. Not just alive. She really was intelligent, like a human being.

But he kept thinking of Cassie walking into the lab, Cassie surprising the burglars...

Jordan pedaled faster.

Cassie picked herself up slowly, leaving bloody hand-prints on the wall. She felt as though she might throw up, but she didn't. She stood in the lab doorway, staring.

The lights were still on, making the windowless room bright as day. Baby lay on the floor, a sad and pathetic lion head, its cables pulled loose. Everything from her desk was on the floor, and so was much of the stuff from the benches: all her tools, the leftover oddments of wire and cables and cards. The big bin of metal scraps was tipped over, her soldering iron and the coffeemaker lay tangled together. The coffee pot itself was broken.

And the covers were off every single computer. Wires trailed. Cassie limped over to look at the nearest, knowing what she would find. The hard drive, with all her stored data, all the information on Baby's development, was gone. Two years of her life. True, the backup of the latest version of her thesis was on a flash drive in her backpack, but the committee reading it would want to see Baby in action too. They weren't going to give her very good marks if they couldn't see the actual proof that her emotion-recognition software did what she said it said.

The recordable DVDs were gone from the shelf. So were all her opera CDs, as though the thieves couldn't tell the difference. All the printouts of her notes, which had been in carefully labeled file folders, were gone. Everything.

She went back to pick up Baby's head. At least they hadn't taken that, but part of the robot's brains, if you wanted to call them that, were the programs in the computer, and those were gone, along with any record of them. Cassie went back to her desk with Baby tucked under her arm. She straightened the phone and dialed 211 for the university security office.

The phone was still plugged in, but the line was dead. Cell phone. Clipped to her belt. She should have called first, as soon as she saw the light under the door. She pulled it off, flipped it open and stared blankly at the cracked screen. Thumbed it on. Nothing. The phone had been under her hip when she fell. Still holding Baby, Cassie limped down the hall to the elevators and went up to the ground floor, out the main doors. There was a phone in a bright yellow metal box on the wall, a direct line to the one security person on the night shift. It began to ring as soon as she lifted the receiver, but it took ages for anyone to answer.

"It's Cassie O'Blenis in computer science," she said when a bored voice finally responded, yawning. "There's been a burglary. Everything in my lab's gone. You'd better call the police."

Then she sat down on the ground by the door to wait. Cassie couldn't help it. She started to cry.

Security was useless. The little officer on duty made tut-tut noises and told Cassie to make a list of everything that was missing. Then he put a padlock on the lab door and told her to go home.

"Call the police," Cassie said, and Jordan, who had arrived at about the same time as security, nodded vigorously.

"Yes, yes. I'll get in touch with Administration and we'll take care of all that. Don't you worry about it. That's Dr. Ruggles's problem, not yours. I'll write a complete report on the damage here, and I'm sure he'll take it very seriously."

"I bet," said Jordan under his breath.

"I don't understand why the alarm didn't go off when this was smashed," the officer added, poking at the electronic lock. "Must be faulty, I guess."

"My phone's dead too," said Cassie. "Someone's tampered with the wires."

"Or the switching system," said Jordan.

The officer smiled indulgently at them. "Why don't we leave that for the experts, eh? You should both be home in bed. Get along, now. Don't worry. It'll all be taken care of."

"What are you doing here?" Cassie asked dully as they got their bicycles. She had paper towels wrapped around her hand so she could hold the handlebars, and Baby's head was clamped on the carrier over the back wheel.

"Cassandra woke me up," Jordan said. "She said there were men in the lab."

"Cassandra woke you up?"

"Yeah, she rang the phone and stuff. I had Baby hooked up for her so she could see things through its eyes. Cameras. Whatever."

"She saw the men?"

"Yeah. She was burning a DVD of her recording when I left. You could give it to the police or something. Um, but we'd better make up some sort of story about how you recorded it."

Cassie didn't really seem to be listening. "The robot's completely wrecked," she said, and her voice was trembling. "They got everything except the head, and that'd be the easiest part to rebuild. It'll take me months. It'll mean an extra year to finish my degree, a whole extra year of my life. I don't understand why..." and her words were lost in a sob.

It was scary. Jordan didn't think he'd ever seen Cassie cry before, except when their grandmother died.

"Don't cry," he said, and his own voice wobbled. "The police can catch them. We've got pictures of their faces."

Cassie sniffed. "Yeah. Right. Sorry. I just..."

"It's all right. Look, are you hungry? Why don't we get a pizza or something? I'm not going to be able to sleep after this, and you looked pretty sick in there. You should eat something."

"Yeah," Cassie said.

"And I have to tell Cassandra I'm back, or she'll wake up Helen."

In the morning there was a meeting in Dr. Ruggles' office. The vice-president and Ms. Dormer were there, of course, and Cassie and Dr. Chan-Fisher. Whenever anything went wrong or people wanted funding for some new project, it always *was* Dr. Ruggles they had to see, not the university president. Everyone knew that, somehow or other, it was Vice-President Ruggles who made all the decisions.

"Have the police looked at the lab yet?" Cassie demanded, even before she sat down in the hard chair Ms. Dormer hadn't offered.

"There's no need to call in the police," Dr. Ruggles said, leaning back in his chair, its leather cushions squeaking. "Campus security is already investigating."

"That's ridiculous!" said Dr. Chan-Fisher. "This isn't a matter for campus security. Thousands of dollars worth of equipment is missing, not to mention all Cassie's work. And on top of that, Cassie was attacked and injured."

Ms. Dormer looked at Cassie's bandaged hand and sniffed, as though she thought it was all a put-on. Dr. Ruggles was smiling.

"You can't mean to tell me you're going to ignore this!" Dr. Chan-Fisher was so angry she jumped up and shook a finger at Dr. Ruggles. "You don't find this funny!"

"Please sit down, Naomi. I don't think you want the police called in at this point. Think of the circumstances. Here is a student I only yesterday reprimanded and threatened with expulsion, and of all the computers on campus, someone decides to steal the ones only she uses? Someone decides to vandalize university property in a locked room that only she and security can access? I really feel that at this point it would be inadvisable to bring this matter to the attention of the police. In fact, I would like to suggest that if the missing equipment—which, I might add, is university property, not yours or Ms. O'Blenis's—is restored promptly, nothing more will be said. And perhaps it might be wise if Ms. O'Blenis turned in her keys to the building. I have never approved of faculty and graduate students being able to enter buildings after hours, and this incident demonstrates that my opinion is justified. I will bring it up before the senate."

"What?" roared Dr. Chan-Fisher. "Are you saying you think Cassie did this herself? You—you—you pompous little twit! You—you—you mush-brained *manager!*"

She tugged at Cassie's sleeve, and Cassie, stunned, jumped to her feet and followed Dr. Chan-Fisher out of the room.

"Wow," she said as her supervisor slammed the door of the outer office behind them. "Good thing he can't fire you."

"Oh my." Dr. Chan-Fisher rubbed trembling hands over her face. "I can't believe I said that. I can't believe I did that." She glanced back over her shoulder at the door. "He's going to make life very unpleasant for us now."

"It can't get much worse," Cassie muttered.

Dr. Chan-Fisher patted her arm. "Come on. Let's go down to the faculty club. We both could use a nice cup of tea." She gave quite a nasty smile, for such a kind-looking woman. "And a little gossip too. Bound to be someone around who'll be interested to hear how very seriously Ruggles takes theft and vandalism and an attack on a student."

Cassie almost smiled. There were always a few professors sitting around in the faculty club, muttering to one another about Dr. Ruggles and his budget cutbacks and endless memos.

Dr. Chan-Fisher was still fuming, though. "Really, Ruggles has gone too far this time. Accusing you!"

"It seems to me he wasn't nearly as surprised as he should have been about the burglary," Cassie remarked, half to herself.

"Don't go saying that in public, Cassie. We have to stick to the facts. They're quite strong enough on their own." Dr. Chan-Fisher shrugged. "Of course, if people think of it on their own..." She smiled happily.

But it was true, Cassie thought. Ruggles hadn't really looked surprised. Of course he'd had the report the security office had written, but still...he'd been prepared to meet with them at nine in the morning. She would have bet he hadn't even had time to actually read the security report.

And she could think of one thing someone might have been looking for in her lab, someone who'd overheard talk about Cassandra, someone who always wanted to know everything that went on at Muddphaug and would even snoop in people's desks to find out.

In her backpack she had the DVD of the burglars that Cassandra had recorded. She hadn't mentioned it to Dr. Chan-Fisher yet. Now she wasn't sure if she should. Dr. Chan-Fisher would use it to make Dr. Ruggles call in the police, but if Dr. Ruggles was behind the burglary, he might realize that the recording was proof of Cassandra's existence.

Cassie decided to wait a few days to see what Dr. Ruggles did next.

Red-tie and Blue-tie

Dr. Ruggles did nothing. Of course. Cassie and Dr. Chan-Fisher cleaned up the robot lab. Maintenance put a new lock on the door and repaired the phone. Cassie changed the lock code to one that Dr. Ruggles wouldn't be able to get from Security, and she put a bolt on the inside too, so that at least no one could come in when she was working. But there wasn't much to do. She spent most of her time in the grad lab upstairs, staring glumly at fractal screensavers. When she came home she sat downstairs watching TV. She didn't talk much.

"Depressed," said Helen. "She's depressed."

"Of course she's depressed," Jordan said angrily. "Her robot got smashed up, she got hurt and old Ruggles is saying she did it all herself. And did you see what was in the paper? *Vandalism at*

Muddphaug U. Disgruntled student suspected. 'The university is dealing with the matter internally,' says VP Ruggles. 'We're making every effort to provide counseling for the suspect.' Counseling!"

"I'd like to see him try," said Helen, and for a moment they both grinned at the thought of Ruggles sending a counselor to talk to Cassie about the feelings that had supposedly made her trash her lab. "Can she sue him for libel, for saying she's a disgruntled vandal?"

"No. He's never actually accused her personally, not in print."

"Too bad."

"Too bad he wouldn't try to expel her," Jordan said thoughtfully. "Then the faculty and the students' union would make a fuss and maybe prove that Ruggles is an idiot."

"He won't," said Helen. "He doesn't want to expel her. He just wants her to think he might. It's a kind of blackmail, to scare her into giving him Cassandra."

"Except probably now he thinks he's got Cassandra," Jordan muttered, and they both sank into sympathetic gloom on Cassie's behalf again.

Two days later, Jordan watched Cassandra's recording of the break-in again. The most useful bit was when the men opened the door and switched on the lights. Baby was still on the shelf then, so there was a good image of their faces. They were both big men. One was thin and one wasn't. They both had bushy mustaches and dark suits. They didn't look like burglars to Jordan—they didn't creep around looking guilty or nervous. They walked right in and started grabbing stuff. Then one of them, with fingers like overstuffed sausages in surgical gloves, grabbed the robot head and dropped it on the floor. He hadn't disconnected the cables yet, so Baby went on watching from the floor for a minute more, until they did rip out the cables.

NickAjaxMorg, Jordan typed. Cassandra, can you check prison records and stuff and look for the two burglars?

Yes, Cassandra answered, and about thirty seconds later she asked, I have found them. Would you like to see?

But outside he heard the grumble of a gasoline engine, the crunch of gravel in the driveway and, as the engine died, the slam of a car door.

Wait, he typed. Someone's here. I'll be back. He closed both the video of the burglary and Cassandra's interface and went to peer out the window. Parked in the driveway was a big white Crown Vic—the last generation of the V-8 gas-guzzlers. The red lights were hidden behind the tinted glass of the back window and the windshield. Only the police drove those big interceptors anymore. Even their new Crown Vics were hybrids, switching between gas or ethanol mix and fuel cells. Jordan knew this old ghost car personally—sort of. It usually sat in the parking lot behind the police station, where he saw it every day on his shortcut to school. The police only fired it up when they really wanted highway power and old-fashioned acceleration. It was easy to recognize by its torn front bumper: a dump truck had run into it and someone had bolted it back together. Seeing it here gave him a tight feeling in his stomach. Cassie was at the university, and Helen and Ajax were off messing around in the stream, so he was all alone in the house. Cats didn't count at a time like this.

The doorbell rang. Jordan went downstairs slowly. Baby was sitting on the dining room table. He grabbed the robot head and shoved it in the bottom of the sideboard, with the lace tablecloth and the holly-patterned Christmas serving dishes. Then he opened the door.

It wasn't the police. It was two big men with bushy mustaches and suits. And somehow he wasn't surprised.

One wore a red tie and one a blue.

"I'm sorry," Jordan said brightly. "We're Catholics. Good-bye." He started to close the door again, but there was a shiny dress shoe in the way.

The man belonging to the shoe laughed. "He thinks we're Mormons. Cute. But we're not, sonny. You'd be Jordan O'Blenis."

"Yes," Jordan said.

"Can we come in?"

"I'm not supposed to let anyone in."

"Well, that's right, that's good. But we're friends of Dr. Fisher-Chin. You know her, don't you? Didn't she tell you we'd be dropping by?"

Liar, Jordan thought. Can't even get her name right.

"No," he said.

"Well, she meant to. She must have forgotten. You know what these professors are like."

"No," he said pointedly. "I don't.

"We're from Bytowne Software Development. Dr. Fisher-Chin mentioned you were quite a hot little programmer. She said you had some things we might want to take a look at."

"Oh," said Jordan, thinking quickly and gritting his teeth at *hot little programmer*. "You're games developers, are you?"

"That's right. Can we come in?"

Blue-tie, who was the one with sausage-like fingers, was leaning on the door as he spoke, so that Jordan, still holding the door, slid slowly backward. Then the men were in, just as though he'd invited them. Red-tie looked around.

Jordan tried to stay calm. These men had hurt Cassie and he wanted to scream at them, kick them and run away and call the police, but they were already in the house, they'd arrived in a police car and they obviously thought they could fool him into telling them whatever they wanted. Fisher-Chin, yeah, right. If he was smart, he might be able to learn something from

them. Like who they really were. Not town police—he
knew all those men and women, at least by sight—and
these two weren't from the local Mountie detachment
either, that was for sure. Jordan led the way into the
living room, where there was not a computer in sight.
The cats were there, though.

Blue-tie plunked himself down in the middle of the
couch. Red-tie sat in Dr. LeBlanc's favorite armchair,
lifting Morg onto his lap.

"What a pretty cat," he said. "Are you a pretty kitty,
hmm?"

Morg, who didn't like strangers any better than he
liked Ajax, hissed and scratched the man before bolt-
ing out of the room.

Red-tie sucked his hand, still trying to smile.

Jordan pretended not to have noticed. He picked
up Nick and stood in front of the fireplace stroking
her, trying to look cute and innocent. Her purring
was comforting.

"Why don't you tell us about the software you've
developed?" Blue-tie said. "You look like a smart guy.
I bet you've done some real cool things."

"I'm really not much good," Jordan said, trying to sound bashful. "I mean, I'm better than the
kids at school. But I don't think I've done anything
that anybody'd really want to play. I'm pretty sure
Dr.—um—Fisher-Chin just tries to encourage me, to
be nice."

"What sort of games have you made?" Red-tie asked.

"Well, there's Ponkles," said Jordan. "It's a sort of a maze, see, a ruined city, and two armies of wizards, and some knights, they're like chess knights, really, just a horse head, all different colors, and then there's the trap doors...it's not really that interesting. It crashes all the time."

He started to make up a lot of technical-sounding nonsense about why the game was really no good, and watching the mustaches nodding like they understood, their eyes glazing over. If they'd really understood anything about programming, they'd have known he was talking rubbish.

"At least," he ended, "that's what my sister says. I don't really know. Like, I just mess around with it."

"What about other programs?" Blue-tie asked. "Dr. Fisher-Chin says you've written quite a nifty little e-mail program."

"Are you sure she said me? I wouldn't know how to do that. It'd be pretty cool if I could."

"Oh well," said Red-tie, with a meaningful look at Blue-tie. "It's too bad you don't have anything you want to show us. You could probably make a lot of money if you'd written a new e-mail program."

They seemed to have forgotten about being game developers.

"Yeah," said Jordan. "Maybe even a thousand dollars, eh?"

"Maybe," said Blue-tie hopefully. "Maybe even more than that."

Jordan shook his head. "Sorry. Like I said, I just mess around."

Red-tie shook his hand and gave him a card. "Call us if you think of anything you'd like to show us."

Jordan locked the door behind them and looked at the card.

John Smith, it said, followed by a cell phone number. That was all.

"Yeah, right," he said aloud. "*John Smith*? Who's really called John Smith?"

Jordan started back upstairs. Then he realized he could hear Ajax barking and ran down again. The barking was coming from the backyard, but when he went out and looked around, there was no sign of Helen. Her bike was gone too. The door of the tool-shed thumped and rattled, as if, just maybe, there was a very large husky inside flinging himself at it. When Jordan hauled the door open, Ajax burst out and ran around the yard, sniffing. Jordan caught his trailing leash. Helen's backpack was in the toolshed too.

But Helen was not, and neither was her bicycle.

Jordan dragged Ajax into the house.

Ajax wouldn't let anyone touch Helen. He had to stay calm and think.

They wouldn't kidnap Helen's *bicycle*. Would they? No. He wasn't going to do anything stupid, like freak out and phone Cassie or Dr. Chan-Fisher. He could think of dozens of reasons Helen might lock Ajax in the shed and ride away.

Actually, he couldn't think of any. And of course, being Helen, her cell phone was probably at the bottom of her backpack, under all the field guides and nets and jars, not anywhere useful, like in her pocket. He took a quick look. Yep, there it was. Fully charged and utterly useless, at least for calling Helen.

But they wouldn't kidnap her and take her bicycle.

Jordan went back up to his room with Ajax whining and nosing at him, demanding to know what he'd done with Helen.

NickAjaxMorg I'm back, he typed into Cassandra's interface. **Show me what you found.**

He sat reading the files that she displayed, his mouth open in amazement.

"Oh wow," he said at last. "Oh boy. We're really in trouble now."

Helen stood up, pedaling hard uphill. After seeing the white car leaving Jordan's driveway, she had taken her bike and followed it all the way through town, but it had left her behind on this last hill on Marsh Street, heading out to the highway. If they were leaving town there was no way she could chase them farther. But she had their license plate number at least, whatever good that would do. She was pretty sure it was a cop car.

She crested the hill and let out a whoop of delight.

"Gotcha, creepazoids!"

The white car was turning in at the Riverview Motel, which had a view, not of the muddy Easter River and the bay, but of the four-lane highway.

Helen coasted down the hill and past the Riverview. The car was parked outside room number sixteen. She went all the way to the gas station, in case they'd seen her following, and found enough change in her pocket to celebrate with a licorice ice-cream cone.

Then she rode back to Jordan's house. He'd obviously let Ajax out of the shed, which was just as well. Ajax could probably do a lot of damage to a flimsy plywood shed.

"Hey, Igor!" she shouted, running up the stairs and dodging out of the husky's way as he came galloping to meet her, making a happy "Mmph, mmph" noise. "Igor? I found them!"

"So did I," said Jordan from the doorway of his room. "Come see."

Don't Try This at Home

"Bureau 6 employee records? I've never heard of Bureau 6," Helen said.

"I have," said Jordan. "I think. There's Bureau 6 and Bureau 7. They're both security agencies—spies, you know. I think Bureau 6 is supposed to do the spying on other people, and Bureau 7 is supposed to stop other people spying on us. Or something like that. Espionage and counterespionage."

"So why is Bureau 6 snooping around here? We're hardly 'other people'—this is our own country," Helen said indignantly.

"Probably once you start spying on people, it's hard to stop. There was just something on the news. Some sort of scandal or something. Bureau 6 was bugging the office of the director of Bureau 7 and they got caught."

"Spies spying on spies. You'd think that would keep them busy and out of trouble. What do spies want with Cassie's hard drives?"

"Cassandra," said Jordan. "Think about it. She reads *everything*."

"All the e-mail in the world? Yeah, I can see why they'd want that, I guess."

"More than that. All the encrypted stuff, since someone always has to decrypt it. Everything. Secret files. Anything that goes through a computer at all, because Cassandra's smart enough now to get herself into any computer, anywhere, any one that's not totally isolated."

"With Cassandra, they could watch everybody."

"Other governments."

"Radical environmentalists."

"Protest groups."

"But how did they find out?"

Jordan pointed at the screen, where Cassandra was still displaying Bureau 6's classified employee records.

"Read that again."

"Reuben Harvey," read Helen. "And Harvey *Dormer!* Boy, this Igor dumb. It didn't sink in the first time. He must be some relation to skeleton-Dormer. She and old Ruggles were eavesdropping, and she told the family spy!"

"The question is, now what do we do?" Jordan asked. "We have the recording. We can prove they trashed Cassie's lab. We can't go to the police. They came in a police car, so they must be working with the police. But we still have to stop them. If our government is willing to do illegal things to get its hands on Cassandra, what would it do if it actually controlled her?"

"And just think about what other governments—dictators and stuff—might do with her," Helen added.

"Um—of course, we probably are breaking the law ourselves, reading things with Cassandra."

"But we haven't, lately. We've stopped."

They both looked at the confidential employee records and started laughing.

"It's an emergency," said Helen. "And anyway, it was against the law for them to break into Cassie's lab and steal stuff in the first place. Spies should have to obey the law like everyone else. Don't they?"

"The thing is," Jordan said soberly. "The thing is, the right thing to do would be to delete Cassandra." He dropped his voice as though the program might hear.

"But she's alive," Helen said, shocked.

"I know. But all the things she can do are wrong. Mostly, that's what she turns out to be best for. Spying on people's private stuff. And you know the government, any government, isn't going to just ignore something like that. They'll say it's against the law, but probably they'll secretly keep her and use her anyway, or sell her to someone who will."

"But we can't delete her. That'd be murder. She's a *person* now. She's alive and self-aware, sentient—she's intelligent and she thinks."

"I know. So what do we do?"

"We make sure Harvey and Harvey don't get her."

"There'll be pieces of her on a lot of hard drives everywhere, now. Including the ones they took from Cassie. But they won't recognize them as anything important, if they find them at all. And they won't be able to make another Cassandra from them, not from just pieces."

"That's good, then."

"They'll keep looking, though."

"Well, we can worry about that later." Helen grinned. "I thought of something we can do for Cassie, anyway."

"What?"

"Get her stuff back. Give me the phone."

Jordan watched Helen dialing.

"Mum? Hi, Mum, it's me. Jordan and I were just thinking, Cassie's pretty down right now. We thought maybe you could take her out for dinner tonight to cheer her up, like to the Lord Muddphaug Inn's dining room or someplace nice like that." Helen listened a bit, nodding, then gave Jordan a thumbs-up. "We'll be fine. There's tons of food around here. Have a good time." She hung up. "That's them out of the way. And in a restaurant there'll be lots of people who can give them an alibi, so we won't get Cassie into any more trouble."

"What sort of trouble?" Jordan asked, starting to frown. This was impressively devious, even for Helen. "What are we doing?"

"This is really, really illegal," Jordan whispered. "We could go to jail."

"No way. We're minors. Juveniles."

"Yeah, juvenile delinquents."

"Well, we are. Anyway, they stole the stuff first. We're just taking it back. Besides, Jordan, think about this. In those hard drives they took, there's a recording of your great True Confession to Baby, about how you wrote Cassandra. You want the government to see that?"

"Okay, okay. But they won't let you have frogs in jail, you know. Just remember that."

The Riverview Motel was a long row of single-story rooms, each with a picture window in front. Helen and Jordan had waited at the end of the street, hidden, they hoped, behind some bushes, and had seen the two Bureau 6 men leave their room and walk along the front of the motel to the adjoining restaurant. Then, walking their bikes, they had hurried down over the steep bank of the roadside and around behind the motel. The back side of the Riverview, which faced the mudflats of the river, had a row of small, square, high windows.

"Sixteen," said Helen, who had been counting even while she argued with Jordan. "Here we are."

"What if they come out of the restaurant?"

"Have you ever eaten at the Riverview Grille? It's the slowest service in town. They won't even have their steak platters yet. Now give me a boost."

Jordan made a stirrup of his hands and heaved Helen up. She set to work with a screwdriver, prying off the window screen.

"What if it's the wrong room?"

"It isn't. I can see a suit hanging up."

"Lots of people wear suits. Ow!"

"Sorry." Helen jumped down and kicked aside the screen, which had hit Jordan on the head as it fell. "Are you coming in, or do I have to do this myself?"

"Lead on, Igor."

They heaved themselves up and through the window, into a bathtub. They both carried big empty backpacks. Jordan's heart was pounding and he kept breaking into fits of shivers. If they were caught...they might not go to prison, but there were youth detention centers. His parents would be summoned back from Belize. He couldn't imagine what they'd say. And anyway, if they were caught, everything would be found out. They couldn't explain what they were doing without explaining Cassandra.

"All clear," said Helen smugly, peering out of the bathroom. "And it is the right room. Clever Igor can count to sixteen."

Jordan edged past her to fasten the chain on the door so no one would be able to come in.

The heavy drapes were drawn over the front window, and in the dim purplish light it was clear that the Bureau 6 agents had been gloating over their trophies. Most of the equipment from Cassie's lab was scattered over the beds.

"Is that laptop hers?" Helen asked.

"No. They must have been reading the disks on it."

"Wonder what they made of this one?" Helen asked, holding up *The Magic Flute*. "Bet they thought it was some sort of encryption. Secret codes."

"Yeah, well, that's opera for you. Stop talking. Someone'll hear. And be careful with the hard drives." Jordan was packing computer parts and disks—both CDs and DVDs—into the backpack, trying to fit them in so they wouldn't rattle around.

"We've got lots of time," Helen repeated, but she started hurrying too.

"I think that's it." Jordan made a final check inside the hockey bag the spies had used to carry Cassie's stuff away, and he looked under the beds.

"Igor miss one," said Helen, and she popped a CD out of the laptop's drive.

"Come on!" Jordan peered out through a gap in the curtain, then took the chain off the door. Helen was already lowering the backpacks out the bathroom window.

She scrambled out. Jordan followed her. He boosted her up again so she could slide the window shut and wedge the screen back on.

"Hurry up, hurry up," he moaned.

Helen gave the screen one final blow with the handle of the screwdriver and slid down. They struggled into the backpacks and walked their bikes through the long grass between the motel and the river. There was a flattened path there already, where people rode illegal, gas-wasting ATVs, so their bicycles didn't leave any tracks. Once they were past the motel they pushed the bikes back up to the road and started riding.

Jordan felt like he had a huge sign over him saying "Thief!" But the things were Cassie's. At least, the disks were, and the work was. And the drives were the university's. And Ruggles wasn't the university; just because he'd told government agents to steal stuff didn't mean they were allowed to.

The pack was heavy and made him wobble.

They were just coming up to the traffic lights when Helen, who was behind him, yelped.

"Jordan!"

He couldn't really turn to look back, not without tipping over, but he ducked his head and looked along his side.

"That's them!"

He couldn't see. Helen was in the way.

"Where?"

"Two blocks back."

Jordan didn't bother waiting for the lights. He turned right, getting up speed on a downhill slope.

Helen pedaled up beside him. She looked scared now, not nearly so certain they could get away with their burglary. "It's a big white car, stuck behind that old man who drives an electric Bug and never goes over twenty. It's got to be them."

Jordan nodded. But he was mad on top of scared now. No way was he letting Harvey and Harvey have Cassie's work, not after all this.

"University," panted Helen. "Mum's office."

"No. They'd just make her give everything back to them. Anyway..." He looked back again. The Crown Vic was heading through the intersection, bumper to bumper with the Bug. It suddenly braked and swung sharply to the right. "They've seen us. We'll never make it to campus anyway."

Jordan pulled ahead again and his bike wobbled as he went around another corner, almost skidding over. Too fast. His heart pounded, and he glanced back to make sure Helen was still behind him. The backpack nearly pulled him over then, and he had to put a foot down to catch himself. He had a brief glimpse of Helen, wobbling from side to side, her teeth bared, as the menacing white car came into view again behind them.

Jordan lowered his head and pedaled harder. What a mess. But he wasn't sure what he could have done differently, to avoid it.

He wondered, yet again, if they put you in jail for stealing something that was your own in the first place. Well, sort of your own, anyway.

He wondered if breaking into the spies' motel room would count as treason, and what they did to you for that.

He made a sharp left, into a neighborhood of mostly old houses, and then took the first turn again, Helen right behind him. For a few moments they were out of sight of Harvey and Harvey.

"Where can we go? Where can we hide? They'll catch us..."

Jordan rode up a driveway, through a backyard. Somewhere out on the street, tires squealed as a car took a turn too quickly. He cut across the yard beyond and out into the next street, then turned up another driveway, whipping out of sight behind the house. He couldn't cut across again—there was a fence along the back. Jordan rode through a flowerbed and into the yard of the next house, which was a modern bungalow made into two apartments. Loud music was blaring from the open back door, but there was no one in sight.

"Quick," Jordan said. "We've got to hide the stuff."

He struggled out of the straps. The windows of the basement apartment were at ground level.

The screen of the closest one was missing, and the window was open.

Jordan reached through and dropped his backpack gently onto the floor, lowering Helen's after it. He had a glimpse of a student-type room, untidy and with shabby furniture. Helen stared open-mouthed.

"Now hurry," he said, and they rode across one more yard and out onto a quiet, tree-lined street.

They zigzagged through a couple more blocks. The prowling white car passed the end of the street they were on twice, but it never turned toward them.

"You know how when you're looking for something, like a book on a shelf, if you get it in your head that it's green and it's actually blue, you can't see it, even when the title's staring you right in the face?" Jordan said once they'd caught their breath.

"Yeah."

"They're looking for big backpacks on bikes. They probably didn't see us at all when they stared down the street just then."

"Good thing, too. It's not like the town's full of Chinese kids and they could mistake me for someone else. Man, the way they came after us...Igor never been so scared."

"They must have found the stuff gone and decided to drive around, to look for anything suspicious."

"Like Mum's truck?"

"Yeah. And they saw two huge backpacks wobbling along and said, *Aha!*"

"Good thing I got Mum and Cassie to go out for dinner, anyway."

Jordan and Helen got all the way back to the O'Blenis house without seeing the white car again. There, they locked all the doors and sat in the living room, eating a bag of chocolate chip cookies with lemonade for supper.

Jordan brought Cassandra's interface up on his laptop and asked her if the spies had sent any messages about the burglary. He had horrible visions of the army showing up to ransack the house.

Harvey Dormer and Reuben Harvey have made no report about any break-and-enter at their motel. They are currently driving up Endor Street.

How do you know? Jordan typed, while Helen, who had been reading over his shoulder, went to check again that the doors were locked, her cell phone clutched in her hand.

Reuben Harvey possesses a satellite phone. I can locate it precisely through the GPS system. They are about to pass 79 Endor Street, driving south.

Jordan went to the window and watched from behind the lace curtains. The white car drove past three times, slowly, but it never turned in.

It was getting dark when Cassie and Dr. Chan-Fisher finally arrived to pick up Helen. They were both fuming. They'd had their dinner, but Dr. Chan-Fisher had gone back to get a book from her office and had found Dr. Ruggles and two men he said were police searching the grad lab.

"And they weren't police at all!" Cassie said. She was shaking, although whether it was with fear or anger was hard to tell. "It was those two goons who trashed my lab and pushed me over! And Ruggles said, dear me, I really was hysterical, perhaps he'd better have security take me to the hospital! So I couldn't say anything more, and they made me let them into the robot lab and they searched it too!"

"And I'm certain they'd already been through my office," Helen's mother said, almost as angry as Cassie. "This is getting out of hand. I'm going to talk to the faculty association. Ruggles has no right to carry on this way." And then she added, with a look that took in all three of them. "I wish I knew exactly what was going on."

Cassie shook her head. She curled up on the couch, looking somehow small and very young.

"We'd better go, Mum," Helen said. "Thanks for supper, Jordan."

"Right," Jordan said. He walked Helen and her mother to the door and locked it after them. Then he turned off all the lights and went back to the living room. He turned off the lights there, too, and looked out the window again. It felt safer in the dark. No one could see in, and he could see the street clearly. Nick rubbed against his ankles, purring. He picked the cat up and put her on Cassie's knees, then sat down beside his sister and patted her shoulder, a bit awkwardly.

"Thanks, kid," she said after a while.

But he didn't tell her about burgling Harvey and Harvey, not yet. Throwing the packs in the basement window had seemed like a good idea at the time, but probably most people, if a bag of computer parts came in their window, would call the police. Which meant Harvey and Harvey might have everything back already. And although he was pretty sure the bungalow's siding had been orange, or some slightly peculiar color at least, he wasn't at all certain he could remember what street it was on.

Frustrate Their Knavish Tricks

"Trouble!" Helen shouted. It was ten in the morning, the day after Jordan and Helen had burgled the spies' motel room.

Jordan ran out of his room and leaned over the banister.

"Harvey and Harvey?"

"Coming up the street. They're turning their blinker on."

Jordan slid down the banister and grabbed his backpack off the hall table. "Right. Got Ajax?"

Helen hurried out of the living room, with Ajax leaping around her on his leash. They raced for the kitchen and out the back door. Jordan locked it behind him. They wormed their way into the dense clump of lilacs beside the garage and sat there, hearts thudding in their chests. Ajax thought it was some new sort of game and kept trying to stick his cold nose in their ears.

"Here," Helen whispered, pulling a handful of dog biscuits out of her pocket. "To keep him quiet."

The Crown Vic pulled into the driveway and drove up right beside the garage.

Ajax leapt to his feet, quivering, and Helen grabbed him around the muzzle.

"No," she whispered. "Quiet. Lie down."

Ajax whined, but he lay down, trying to get as much of himself as possible onto her lap. Helen fed him biscuit after biscuit as the Bureau 6 men got out of the car, looked around and walked to the back door.

Jordan had been expecting this. Someone had been phoning the O'Blenis house every five minutes for the last half hour. They hadn't answered it. Cassandra had traced the calls for them and said they came from Reuben Harvey's phone.

Harvey and Harvey had been checking to make sure nobody was home.

Now, while Red-tie stood looking around the yard, Blue-tie bent down and fiddled with the lock. In a moment they had the door open.

Nick shot out between Blue-tie's feet, making him stumble.

Ajax whined again, catching sight of Nick, who sat in the middle of the yard, staring at the strange car. The cat looked around at the bush, then started to wash her face.

"Quiet," Helen repeated.

They waited and waited.

"If they take anything..." Jordan whispered. "If they wreck anything..." He was beginning to doubt his plan. "They trashed the lab."

"They wanted it to look like real burglars that time."

"Well, they might here too."

"I bet that would look too suspicious, two burglaries of the same person's things. They won't want to leave any evidence this time. They think if they steal Cassie's stuff back from us, we won't dare go to the police, because we stole it from them. But if the house was trashed, of course we would. Jordan!"

"What?"

"The robot head! They'll look in the sideboard, anybody would."

"They didn't take it when it was in the lab—anyway, it's not in the sideboard anymore."

"Where is it?"

"I buried it at the bottom of the clothes hamper."

"Oh. When was the last time Cassie did laundry?"

"Mmm. A while ago. She bought some new socks and underpants for me so we could go longer without doing the wash. I think it's probably been at least two weeks."

"Oh. I guess Baby's safe then. If it doesn't melt from sock fumes."

"Shh," Jordan said, watching a man's head move past his open bedroom window. He clenched his hands into fists. "How long have they been in there?"

"Twenty minutes," said Helen.

"That's enough time. It must be obvious the stuff isn't there." Jordan dragged the laptop out of his backpack, typed **Now, Cassandra!** into the interface and then took out his cell phone.

"What are you doing?"

"Igor and Cassandra make cunning plan."

He dialed 911.

"Hello?" he said when someone answered. "Hello? I need the police." He made his voice weak and quavery, trying to sound like an old lady. "I think my neighbors are being robbed! There's a white car in the yard, and two men went into the house, and I know there's nobody home. 79 Endor Street. Hurry!" And he hung up before they could ask his name again.

Helen was making horrified faces. "Idiot Igor! They can trace cell phone numbers, you know. And they'll call back."

"Idiot Igor. Cassandra can fake information, you know. They'll get a busy signal when they call the number they think this came from. And they'll have to come check the report out, just in case."

"Oh." Helen made another face. "You're a lousy parent. Now you've taught her to lie."

It didn't take the town police long to arrive. They pulled silently into the driveway in a hybrid-engine Crown Vic, blocking the spies' car. Two officers got out, just in time to meet Harvey and Harvey coming empty-handed from the back of the house.

The two Bureau 6 men stopped. So did the police.

"Oh," said one of the officers—Jordan recognized her, Sergeant Suzie Cowan. "It's you. We've had a complaint...I thought you were investigating industrial espionage down at the university?" She sounded awfully suspicious for a woman talking to her colleagues in law enforcement.

"Quiet," Helen whispered in Ajax's ear. He was whining again. Blue-tie looked around, but he didn't see them.

"Ah," said Red-tie, frowning. "Nothing you need to worry about. Everything's in order."

"Is it?" asked Cowan's partner, Al Furlong.

Blue-tie sighed and pulled a folded paper from his pocket. "Inter-departmental cooperation, remember?" he said.

The two police officers read the paper, their heads together, frowning. Some sort of search warrant, Jordan guessed. Cowan went around to check the back door.

"Unlocked," she said, with a suspicious scowl at Blue-tie. "The O'Blenises are away, aren't they? I knocked, but there's no answer."

"The kids are still in town," Furlong said, handing him the paper. "What's all this about, then? What do the O'Blenises have to do with industrial espionage?"

"I'm afraid that's all you need to know," said Blue-tie, rather smugly. "National security. Now if you wouldn't mind moving your car, we'll be on our way. You don't want to cause a disturbance."

Suzie Cowan muttered something under her breath that sounded like "On your way in *our* car, and why you spooks can't rent one, like ordinary people, instead of using up our gasoline credits..." She stood scowling in the driveway until Furlong honked the horn at her. Then she joined her partner and they backed out into the street. It looked like they were arguing. Suzie Cowan was known to be a bit hot-tempered, as well as very fond of driving the old interceptor very fast to impress young male officers. Probably she was all for arresting the spies then and there—for playing with her favorite toy, if nothing else.

"Prying neighbors," muttered Red-tie, glaring at the house next door. "No privacy anywhere these days. I don't know what the world's coming to."

"Now what?" Blue-tie asked. "What have they done with those drives and disks? They're not at the university. They're not here."

"Maybe it wasn't the kids after all. Maybe Ruggles had a better offer for the data."

"Dolores would have told me."

"Maybe she had a better offer."

"She's my sister!"

"So maybe Ruggles didn't tell her he had a better offer. Let's try his house."

They drove away, and Helen let Ajax go. He raced

around the yard, barking. Nick bolted up a lilac trunk and sat on the garage roof, spitting at him.

When they went back inside, the phone was ringing. This time Jordan did answer it.

"Jordan, you're all right!" It was Cassie.

"Yeah, sure," he said guiltily. "Shouldn't I be?"

"I just had a call from Al Furlong. He said someone reported a burglary at our house and it turned out to be what he called 'another agency with a warrant,' so there wasn't anything he could do. But he said I should have a look around when I got home, and 'I didn't hear that from him.' He also said to tell you and Helen not to hide in green bushes when you're wearing red."

Jordan grimaced and looked down at his T-shirt. "Harvey and Harvey—um, your burglars, you know—picked the lock and searched the house. I called the police but pretended I was one of the neighbors."

"And you stuck around to watch? Jordan O'Blenis!"

"Don't worry, the Harveys didn't see us, even if Furlong did. And they didn't take anything this time."

"But he said they had a search warrant, like we were criminals or something." Cassie sounded close to tears. "Do you want me to come home?"

"No! No, that's okay. We're okay. We're going to go for a bike ride or something." Jordan hesitated. He didn't want to get Cassie's hopes up, not yet, just in case whoever owned that apartment had thrown all the stuff out or sold it to Bingo's Used Computers or something. "Cassie? It's going to be all right. Don't worry."

"Yeah, right." Cassie sighed. "Well, if you're sure you don't mind being on your own. See you at supper. I think there's a chicken casserole in the freezer, if you could get it out to thaw..."

"Right. Bye." Jordan hung up. "Hey, Igor?"

Helen came back downstairs. "Just checking. Ajax's tracked them through every room in the house."

"Well, that's good. They've looked everywhere, so they won't come back. Let's go find the stuff."

Jack Calvin

Helen and Jordan rode their bikes slowly through the streets they'd crossed the evening before. Ajax ran alongside. It wasn't as hard to find the bungalow as Jordan had feared. There it was, sandwiched in between two big old houses. And it was a sort of dull, faded orange color, just as he'd thought he remembered. They walked their bikes around to the back.

"It'd be easiest if no one was home," said Helen. "We could just go in through that window and take our stuff back."

"You're really getting into this burglary thing, aren't you?"

Helen grinned. "Maybe I'll become an international cat burglar as well as a biologist."

"What would you do with all the cats, though?"

He dodged Helen's punch and walked down the damp, concrete stairs to the basement door. This time the noise spilling out was from a TV. He peered into the grubby kitchen, then pounded hard on the aluminum panel of the screen door. Finally a plump young man wearing nothing but a pair of track pants came into the kitchen.

"Yeah?" he asked, opening the door.

"Um..." Jordan realized he hadn't really thought about what to say.

"We want to talk to whoever lives in that bedroom," said Helen, pointing along the back wall of the house.

"Oh. That's Jack. Go on in." The young man went back to the living room and the TV without another word.

Jordan shrugged and walked into the kitchen. The floor was a bit sticky. Helen wrinkled her nose.

"Students," she said. "Ick. Can you imagine living like this?"

The apartment wasn't very big. There was no sign of their backpacks in the kitchen or in the living room catty-corner to it. The door of the back bedroom was closed. Jordan knocked on it. There was no answer, but the baseball game on the TV was probably too loud for whoever was in the bedroom to be able to hear over it. He knocked a bit harder.

Helen reached around him and turned the knob.

"Helen!"

Ajax pushed past them into the room.

"Gosh, sorry," Helen said in an artificially bright voice, following the husky. "He got away from me."

The unmade bed had a scatter of books over it. More books were stacked along the wall. There was a desk, with a computer and more books, and a bulletin board covered in several layers of handwritten notes, postcards and newspaper clippings. Tacked in the middle was a notice written in red marker. It said, *Eternal vigilance is the price of paranoia.*

"Hello?" said Helen. There was a young man working at the desk, his back to the door. Obviously a student, given the heaps of books all over the room, he was dressed in shorts and a T-shirt. Ajax, after sniffing around the room, put his nose on the young man's bare, hairy leg. That got his attention. He yelped and jumped up. His chair went over with a bang and he leapt again, this time onto the bed.

Ajax started to bark.

"Oh!" he said in relief. "It's just a dog!" He jumped back to the floor and patted Ajax. "Where'd you guys come from?"

For a moment, Jordan was too busy reading his T-shirt to answer. It had aliens on it and read, *My abductors went to Area 51 and all I got was this lousy T-shirt.* He had long brown hair in a ponytail, a goatee and crooked gold-rimmed glasses.

"Your roommate said we should come in," Helen said as she stepped into the room.

"Just a sec." The student pulled a pair of earplugs out of his ears. "Ronnie's always got the TV so loud...what did you say?"

"He...er...Ronnie said we should just come in," said Jordan. "We...um..."

"We threw some stuff in your window last night," Helen said.

"Oh, was that you? I thought it must be thieves chucking their loot. But I didn't hear any sirens."

Jordan turned red and shuffled his feet. "Do you still have it?"

"Yeah." The student scratched his goatee. "You sure it's yours?"

"I know you," Helen said suddenly. "You work in the library."

"Yeah! I've seen you around. You do your homework there every afternoon, don't you? Your mother's a prof. Here, sit down. I'm Jack Calvin." He cleared some books off the bed. "You guys want a beer or something?"

"Sure," said Helen.

"Helen!"

"Oh, right. I thought you looked kind of short for undergrads. Ginger ale?" Jack didn't wait for an answer but went out to the kitchen.

"He might phone the police," Jordan whispered, looking around the small room. "You see the packs?"

"He won't do that, he works in the library," said Helen. "I see him there all the time."

"That doesn't make him your friend."

"Sure it does."

Jack came back with three cans of ginger ale.

"So," he said, handing them around, "I heard a computer lab got robbed. You guys would be the mystery men who beat up the prof and carried away all the computers, right?"

"We didn't..." Jordan started to shout, but Helen elbowed him.

"He's joking," she said. "We just got the stuff back from the thieves."

"Really? Cool."

"And it wasn't a prof," said Jordan, still angry. "It was my sister Cassie. She's a grad student."

"Oh yeah? How'd you guys find the thieves?"

"They went to his house," said Helen, pointing to Jordan. "And I followed them when they left."

"We knew it was them because we had a recording of them trashing the lab."

"Why'd they go to your house, though?"

"They didn't find what they wanted in the lab."

"How'd you know that?"

Somehow, piece by piece, they ended up telling Jack Calvin almost everything.

"Yeah, I know about that," Jack said when they mentioned how Ruggles and Dormer snooped around. "I'm in History, and they're always coming around, poking into things, asking why we have to keep buying more books, saying, 'It isn't like studying history prepares you for today's business environment,' and things like that. Makes the professors froth at the mouth. Really. Well, almost. So you think it's Bureau 6 that's after you?"

"We know it is."

"Bureau 6," Jack said thoughtfully, and searched through the clippings on his bulletin board. "Yeah, they do all sorts of fishy stuff. Illegal wiretaps. Here it is. A Royal Commission looking into accusations that they fiddled the books and bought helicopters for themselves that never showed up in the government accounts."

Jordan and Helen glanced at the cutting politely. It looked very boring.

"It wasn't actually helicopters," said Jack. "They were really using the money to build a base up north to study a crashed UFO."

Jordan groaned. "You believe that stuff?"

"I'm not sure," Jack Calvin said thoughtfully. "It's fun to think about, at least. Helps keep an open mind and all that. But they definitely do go outside the law and do all sorts of things that have no place in a democratic country. What do they want with your sister, though? I don't understand that bit."

"It's not her, it's Cassandra," said Jordan.

"Okay, who's Cassandra?"

Jordan bit his lip.

"We can trust him," Helen said encouragingly. "He works in the *library*."

"Cassandra's a computer program I wrote," Jordan said. "And she's alive. Um, I can show you, if I can use your computer?"

"Knock yourself out," Jack invited with a wave of his hand.

It didn't really matter what kind of program he used. E-mail, a Web browser, instant messaging, a word processor—they were all the same to Cassandra so long as the computer had an Internet connection. Jordan typed Cassandra's codeword, NickAjaxMorg, into the subject field of a search engine. Cassandra's plain text interface popped up instantly.

It's okay, we're getting Cassie's stuff back, he wrote. A history student called Jack Calvin lives here. He wants to talk to you. Can you prove to him that it's not a trick I'm doing?

Hello Jack Calvin, Cassandra replied. We are very glad you did not take Cassie's equipment to the police. We fear it is not safe to trust the police. Bureau 6 has authority to make them "cooperate," which is not a good thing. I do not know what proof you need to believe that I am not a trick. I see that you visit many international news websites, many websites relating to the Industrial Revolution and the eighteenth century, and many sites relating to such subjects as UFOs and conspiracy theories, which I am sorry to say contain information and evidence which I do not find at all factual or convincing. If you put any credence in the information on such sites, I suspect you will believe almost anything and there is no need for me to offer proof of my existence.

Jack scratched his goatee thoughtfully. Then he grinned. "I'm sold," he said. "So, Cassandra, since you're here—can you proofread my thesis for me?"

"She can't hear you," Jordan said, with a sigh of resignation at how computer-ignorant some people could be. "Not now that Baby's not working, not without a mike and the right program..." His voice trailed off, ideas bubbling in his imagination.

"No time for that now, Igor," said Helen, recognizing the danger signs.

"Man," Jack said and shook his head. "No wonder Bureau 6 is after you. You're lucky you don't have the Americans and the French and the Chinese and everybody camped out here."

"They probably haven't heard yet," said Jordan glumly.

"Old Ruggles is probably getting millions for selling her to the government. What are you going to do? They're not going to give up just because you got her back."

"She's not on the drives. All that stuff they took is Cassie's robot work, that's why we had to get it back."

"Robots! Cool!"

"You can't isolate her to just a few computers. Cassandra's everywhere. There's a piece of her installed on your computer."

"Really?" Jack didn't seem very interested in that aspect of it. He certainly didn't act as though she was a virus he wanted removed right away. "Well, anyway, they're not going to quit until they have Cassandra."

"Yeah, I know."

"So what are you going to do?"

"I don't know."

"Count me in, anyway."

"Really?"

"Sure thing. Man, you outsmarted Bureau 6. That's something! Anyway, you want your sister's work back? I just chucked the backpacks in the wardrobe while I decided what to do about them. Um, don't mind the laundry."

Helen removed a pair of dirty socks, very cautiously, and pulled out the backpacks.

"Want a lift home?" Jack asked. "I've got a van. Electric. One of the early ones. Sometimes the engine even starts."

Bonfire of the DVDS

Jack stayed with them all day, as reinforcements in case Harvey and Harvey reappeared, but all was quiet. They poked around the Web a bit. Jack showed them a few sites that, he claimed, monitored Bureau 6. They mostly seemed to be about aliens and orbiting ray guns and weather beams.

"Bunch of nutcases" was Helen's opinion.

Jack grinned. "Probably. But you believe you've been talking to a live computer program."

"We have."

"Exactly. Anyway, they're right about one thing. Bureau 6 thinks it's above the law in this country. And once they have your Cassandra, they'll be able to watch everyone."

"I know," said Jordan. "If she was just a computer program, I'd get rid of her. But she isn't. She's alive."

"So what will you do?" Jack asked. "They won't just give up simply because they can't find your sister's disks."

"I don't know," said Jordan. "I just don't know."

"Come on," Helen said, hearing the misery in his voice and changing the subject. "Let's play—"

Jordan sighed.

"No, not Go." Helen made a fake sympathetic face. "I know it's annoying to lose all the time. I learned that playing against Cassandra. What I was actually going to say was, show Jack your Ponkles game."

They spent the afternoon playing Ponkles. Cassandra broke in and insisted she had to play too. Naturally, she won.

Before supper, Dr. Chan-Fisher arrived to take Helen and Ajax out to Wood Hill, and shortly after they left, Cassie got back.

"Whose van?" she asked, staring suspiciously at Jack as he came down the stairs behind Jordan.

"This is Jack," Jordan explained. "He...um...Helen and I got your stuff back from Harvey and Harvey, and hid it in Jack's house yesterday, and he drove us home today."

"Oh," said Cassie, and then, "What? My stuff? You mean—"

"All the drives, all the data, everything," said Jordan happily. It was like watching someone turn a light on behind Cassie's face. She almost glowed. "Even your operas."

"Wow! How? Where is it?

It took a long time to explain. By the time he was done, she had everything unpacked and was installing her hard drives in Ozy the supercomputer in the upstairs hall, checking that everything was intact.

"But Maman and Dad will kill me if they find out you did anything so stupid while I was looking after you. You could have been caught. You could have been arrested!"

"Well, but…"

"Oh, good, this one's fine too." Cassie wasn't really paying any attention to telling him off, or to his protests. "I was afraid they'd be scratched, with all that rattling around. I'll take everything back to the lab tomorrow. They wouldn't dare rob it twice. What did I do with Baby's head?"

"Baby's head?" asked Jack.

"You didn't do anything with it," Jordan said. "It was in the sideboard, but I moved it. It's hidden under the dirty clothes."

Cassie looked up and made a face. "In that case, I nominate you to go get it."

"Why is a baby's head in the dirty clothes?" Jack asked. "Or is this something I really shouldn't ask?"

"Don't ask," Jordan suggested. "Or, um, do you want to go get it?"

"No."

Jordan sighed and held his breath as he fished for Baby. Really, really time to do some laundry.

"Right," Cassie said, taking the head from him and patting it affectionately. "Okay. Is there a network card around here somewhere?"

"Not so much a baby as a lion that's been chewed on by too many babies. I'll just go do something useful," Jack said. "You guys eat pancakes?"

"Um, sure," said Cassie, lying down on her side to stare into a computer. "Whatever. Jordan, screwdriver."

Jack and Jordan pulled Cassie away from her computers long enough to eat pancakes, and then Jack said goodbye to Jordan and headed home, promising to come back the next day. Cassie was clamping Baby to a chair and hooking up cables to make sure its mechanism hadn't been damaged. Morg, who was stalking past waving his great plumy tail in the air, flattened himself to the floor as the head hummed and the lenses, focusing on him, suddenly whined. He jumped onto a computer and they tracked him. He hissed.

"Hah!" said Cassie. "When I build a robot, I build a tough robot. Guaranteed one hundred percent stinky-sock proof."

Jordan watched Cassie playing with the robot and Morg for a while and then went back to his own room and shut the door. For a while he just sat, with Nick curled up, purring, on his lap.

After a while he typed, NickAjaxMorg. Good morning Cassandra.

Hello Jordan O'Blenis. You use the SETI screensaver. Do you believe in aliens?

Have you been looking at Jack Calvin's files?

He is writing about social disruption and the Industrial Revolution. His thesis shows that he is intelligent and rational and very well-read. He either cannot spell or he is a poor typist. Yet, even though he is intelligent and rational, he collects information on aliens and flying saucers. I do not mean that he reads good science fiction about aliens, although he does, or that he is interested in scientific speculation about life on other planets. I mean he reads articles with headlines like "Two-Headed Space-Alien Pig-Baby Born in Omaha!" I remarked on this when you asked me to prove to him that I was not a prank. This is not rational.

Hobbies are for fun. People relax their minds by playing with silly ideas sometimes. It doesn't mean he really believes in Two-headed Space-Alien Pig-Babies.

But do you believe there could be aliens?

You're sort of an alien. You're intelligent, but you're not human.

But I do not have a flying saucer.

Jordan stared at that for a while.

Was that a joke?

Yes.

Ha ha.

I am glad you liked it.

Do you want to play a joke?

What sort of a joke?

Harvey Dormer and Reuben Harvey are really annoying. And they had no right to steal Cassie's things. And you can control the phones.

Their phones? Cassandra asked.

Yes. Jordan thought for a moment and grinned. Make it so that every time they try to phone someone, it rings their boss's number. Can you do that?

Yes. Is this funny?

I think so. They deserve it.

But it is not right. However, for you I have done it. Jordan O'Blenis, I have found a Bureau 6 report called "The Muddphaug University Cassandra Virus." I believe you should read it, although it is an invasion of privacy to do so, and perhaps theft of intellectual property as well. Perhaps I should not have read Jack Calvin's files. I believe this was wrong of me. I shall send him a note of apology.

Who told you about invasion of privacy? And don't send Jack a note. It would worry him.

It is too late; I have already sent it. As for invasion of privacy, I read many things. I learn. It is what you designed me to do. Would you like to read the Charter of Rights?

Not right now.

I think much of what I do is wrong. I am unsure how to behave. But this report concerns you. Perhaps you should read it. I cannot decide.

So now he had a computer program that was not only alive, but was experiencing ethical dilemmas, worrying about what was right and what was wrong. Great. He wasn't old enough to start being a father and having serious parent-child talks.

I guess the most important thing is not to hurt other people, Jordan typed, thinking about "I am unsure how to behave." **Show me the report. Harvey and Harvey are the ones who started breaking the law.**

The report was fairly short. It had been written by Harvey Dormer and was all about an e-mail surveillance program that could install itself on all the computers in a network and read everything written or stored on those computers. It was important to gain control of this program and prevent its being used by "foreign powers" and "interests contrary to good government."

"That probably means me," Jordan muttered.

The report recommended that Bureau 6 use "any means necessary" to obtain all copies of the program. "To maintain maximum departmental advantage in domestic intelligence, pains must be taken to ensure that Bureau 7 and the RCMP remain unaware of the existence of the Cassandra Virus." They obviously didn't really understand how Cassandra worked. "The program also has applications of great value in the forthcoming BWB operation."

"BWB operation?" Jordan wondered aloud. "Why does that sound familiar?"

Nick just purred blissfully and didn't answer.

"BWB." He tapped the computer's stylus on the desk thoughtfully. "Hah." BWB Aerospace was a company that designed special planes and did a lot of work for the space program. And the project Cassie was supposed to start working on at Prince Albert University in the fall was being funded by BWB.

Not good news, not at all. He did a quick search, but there were no more mentions of BWB in the report. Still...it was a bit worrying.

The report concluded by saying that, if the "Cassandra Virus" could not be obtained for Bureau 6, it was vital, "in the interests of national security," that the program and all documentation relating to it be destroyed.

I do not want to be destroyed, Cassandra wrote. But you have included in my original code a means of deleting me.

Yes.

Do you intend to delete me?

Of course not.

But what did he intend to do? Jack was right: Bureau 6 wasn't going to give up and go home just because they'd lost Cassie's thesis, which wouldn't have been any good to them once they'd read it, anyway. They'd keep trying to get Cassandra. The fact that she wasn't something you could put in a suitcase wouldn't matter. The original code existed. It was on Jordan's computer and on a DVD, and he had a lot of paper notes too, because sometimes he still liked to brainstorm with old-fashioned paper and pencil. If they managed to steal and install the original code, it would spread through the Internet, just as Cassandra had done. It would reach such a size and complexity that it would start to think, just like Cassandra. But Bureau 6 would be the ones telling it what to do.

Let's start by destroying all the records of your existence, Jordan typed. Erase all Bureau 6 files and memos and e-mails and stuff that refer to you.

But it is not right to destroy another person's property.

Cassandra, it will be far worse if Bureau 6 creates another program like you. No one would be able to do anything without the government watching. Sometimes you have to do something that's a little bit bad to keep far worse things from happening. Delete the files!!!

It is done. All Bureau 6 information pertaining to the Cassandra Virus is being deleted. But they may have paper records.

At least they'll be confused.

Anne Polanski of Bureau 6 has now been phoned by Reuben Harvey six times.

Is she their boss? Good.

Ha ha, wrote Cassandra. They were attempting to phone Dolores Dormer, Tommy's Pizza and their phone service provider. Anne Polanski has e-mailed her section chief to enquire if Reuben Harvey has a drinking problem.

!!!

What do we do now?

Jordan sighed. There's only one thing I can think of, he typed. To start with, I have to erase your original code from my hard drive.

"Whatcha doing?" Cassie asked, standing in the back door to peer beyond Jordan into the yard. "It's past time you should be in bed. And what's that awful smell?"

"Disks," said Jordan.

Cassie came out onto the driveway, where Jordan had the charcoal barbecue set up. A fire was blazing in it, not charcoal but dead twigs and paper. Black, oily smoke rose from a lump of melting plastic.

"Disks?" Cassie asked, and took the fork from him to poke at the sheaf of paper. "Oh." She put her arm around him.

"I can't let them get Cassandra," Jordan said.

"Is this all of it, all the hard copy of her code?"

"Every copy," Jordan said. He felt a bit like the ancient Greek king whose daughter had been demanded by the gods as a sacrifice, although of course in the story of the Trojan War it was Iphigenia who was meant to be sacrificed, while Cassandra, who wasn't a Greek at all, was merely carried off to be a slave. Just what Jordon didn't want to happen to his Cassandra. "I guess we should probably talk to Harvey and Harvey, eh? Let them know there's nothing left to steal." he said.

"Yeah," said Cassie. "You know, that program is something I wouldn't have thought of in a hundred years. You shouldn't have done it that way, infecting other people's computers, but you know what they say, 'You can't put the genie back in the bottle.' It's done now."

"Yeah."

"You won't do anything that irresponsible again."

"Probably not," he admitted.

Cassie grinned. "Creating a new life-form is probably a once-in-a-lifetime experience anyway, Dr. Frankenstein."

"Yeah."

"Jordan?"

He looked at her.

"I mean it. I couldn't have done that in a hundred years. I mean, I probably could have done the programming, if I'd thought of it, but I would never have thought of it."

Jordan nodded. The praise felt warm, glowing like the fire, inside him.

"Awful to watch so much work burn," Cassie said after they had stood in friendly silence for a few minutes. "But I think you're doing the right thing. You can't let Harvey and Harvey get it and copy it. Come inside and I'll make you some hot chocolate."

"In a minute," said Jordan. He wanted to watch the fire a while longer.

Confound Their Politics

Jordan wriggled in his chair. He'd never thought a chair could be so uncomfortable. It must have taken some sort of evil engineering genius, to design something so hard with proportions so exactly wrong for the human body.

"It was just a prank," he said, looking down at his hands. "I never thought anyone'd take it seriously. I mean, a program that'd do all that stuff you said, you'd have to be a genius or something to do that. I just wanted to bug my sister, make her think I was reading her e-mail. You know. Because she was so busy working all the time and stuff and not paying any attention to me. Just bug her a bit. I set it up so it'd respond to simple questions with programmed answers. I didn't think anyone else was going to hear about it."

Cassie scowled as though she was mad at what he was saying.

"So it was on the missing hard drives all the time?" said Red-tie.

"Um, no," Jordan said. "It was just a little program. I deleted it from Cassie's computer after a couple of days. I mean, Cassie would have figured out what I was doing if I'd given her time to really look at it."

"I want to see the program," Red-tie said, while Blue-tie rubbed his hands together as though he was dreaming of giving Jordan a good thumping.

"I burned it," said Jordan, looking down at his hands again. "I got scared. All these robberies and stuff, and the police coming around."

"I caught him burning papers and disks last night," Cassie confirmed. "Here." She held out a grocery bag full of shriveled lumps of blackened plastic. "When I asked him what he was doing, he broke down and confessed everything. I wish he'd told me sooner. We could have saved you a lot of time. I knew he was pulling some sort of prank on me, but if I'd known that was what you all were looking for—if you'd only asked me instead of all this sneaking around..."

"I knew it was a mistake to let those children roam the campus unsupervised," Ruggles said, and Ms. Dormer nodded vigorously. "Where's the other one?"

"She didn't have anything to do with it," Jordan said quickly. "She doesn't know anything about computers. You know what girls are like with technical things."

Cassie started to cough behind her hand, and Dr. Chan-Fisher seemed to be screwing up her face to stifle a sneeze. But neither of the Harveys appeared to find anything funny in what he'd said, sitting in a room with two female computer whizzes.

"Anyway," said Cassie, "I saved one copy of the program before I deleted it from his computer. Here." She offered Blue-tie a CD. "You can run it anywhere. It's not very big. It just gets into the e-mail program, like a virus, and generates random smart-aleck comments based on keywords. And if you type in questions in response to the comments, it does the same thing. That's all. If you were really gullible it might fool you into thinking it's reading the mail, but it isn't. Have fun."

Blue-tie took the disk suspiciously.

"That's all?"

"That's all," said Cassie. "Except," she added nastily, "I'm grounding my brat brother for the rest of the summer."

The rest of the summer was one week.

"That, I approve of," said Dr. Ruggles. "From now on, I do not want to see Jordan O'Blenis on campus. Anywhere on campus. If he so much as walks on the lawns, I'll have Security on him."

Yeah, right, thought Jordan, but he didn't say anything aloud.

"Right," said Red-tie. "Well. Thank you for your cooperation, Ms. O'Blenis, Dr. Fisher-Chin. Dr. Ruggles, I must say that although we appreciate the spirit in which you brought this matter to our attention, I'd suggest in future that you make certain of your facts first."

He got to his feet and nodded to Blue-tie, who followed him out with only a nod to his sister, Ms. Dormer.

She sniffed as though to say, good riddance.

"We are *pleased* you eventually decided to come forward with the *facts*, Ms. O'Blenis," Dormer said to Cassie. "But *really*, I must say your *conduct* in this affair does you *no credit*."

"Yes," said Ruggles, steepling his pudgy fingers under his chins. "In future you would do better to come to me at once when you believe you have made a great discovery."

Cassie opened her mouth and then, at a look from Naomi Chan-Fisher, shut it again.

"Yes, Dr. Ruggles," she said meekly. "May we go now?"

"Yes," the vice-president said, and the three of them got up to leave. "And Ms. O'Blenis?"

Cassie turned in the doorway.

"I shall be communicating with your parents today to make sure they understand the seriousness of the trouble their children have caused for Muddphaug."

"Yes, Dr. Ruggles."

"I expect you want to go home for some sort of victory celebration," said Dr. Chan-Fisher once they were out of the administration building. "I'll give you a lift. And Cassie, we should get your data—which Helen tells me has mysteriously reappeared—back to the lab."

"Good thing old Ruggles doesn't have something like Baby running in his office," Cassie muttered to Jordan. "I'd have been hoist by my own petard."

"What?"

"Blown up by my own weapon, that means. Caught by my own lie detector."

Jordan giggled and tried to look serious when he caught Dr. Chan-Fisher's eye on him. Squeezed into the cab of the professor's truck between her and Cassie, he braced himself for an interrogation.

"I don't want to know," Naomi Chan-Fisher said, shifting gears awkwardly, with Jordan's legs in the way. "I don't want to hear the word Cassandra. But I think it wouldn't hurt you to take a nap. You look like you were up all night compiling code."

"Who, us?" Cassie asked and yawned. Jordan giggled again in relief and was elbowed in the ribs.

"Not *all* night," he said. "The thing we made for Harvey and Harvey to look at wasn't that big a program."

"I said I don't want to know." But Dr. Chan-Fisher smiled. "So long as you aren't reading other people's e-mail, and you and Helen haven't got yourselves arrested..."

"And I can get Baby set up in time to show my thesis committee," Cassie said.

"Take that awful scruffy lion head off first," Dr. Chan-Fisher advised.

"How'd it go?" Helen asked as soon as her mother and Cassie had loaded up all the recovered robot stuff and driven away. She sat on the floor with Ajax. Jack sat on the bed with both cats on his lap. Even Morg, who hated being cuddled, had decided, for some reason, that Jack Calvin was the Perfect Human Pillow. Jack said it was because he took fish-oil pills with his morning vitamins to keep his brain young, and maybe the cat recognized another creature with fish-breath. Helen said it was because there was cat-nip growing all around his apartment.

"I'm banned from all university buildings," said Jordan cheerfully. "And Ruggles is going to complain to my parents."

"That's rough," said Jack.

"Naw, they don't check their e-mail more than once a day when they're working in the field. The message will be gone before they ever see it. I'll ask Cassandra to look after it. No point worrying them now that it's all over." He felt a bit guilty about doing that, but a complaint from Ruggles would just upset his parents for no reason. It was for their own good. Of course, that's probably what Harvey and Harvey thought about monitoring other people's mail...Ohhh, power was such a burden. Deleting his parents' e-mail was different from lying to Ruggles and the agents from Bureau 6—that had been to protect Cassandra from being destroyed or, maybe even worse, exploited and used to spy on people's private lives. There weren't any laws to protect a life-form like her, but somebody had to. She was like his child in a way, and he really should be setting a good example. Doing what was right, not just what made his life easier. The responsibility made his head hurt. Maybe he'd better leave the message alone and trust his parents to believe Cassie instead of old Ruggles. And he still hadn't decided whether he should get into the BWB Aerospace computers, to try to figure out why Bureau 6 was interested in them. But if Cassie was going to run into trouble with Bureau 6 again once she was working with BWB Aerospace, then surely it was okay to try to find out what was going on, for Cassie's sake. Ohhh, headache.

"I thought you deleted poor Cassandra," Jack said, distracting him, which was just as well.

"He never said that," said Helen. "He couldn't. It wouldn't be right. She's alive."

"I just deleted the original program from my hard drive and destroyed the copies. Cassandra doesn't actually need it anymore to exist. All I need it for is to remember what I wrote. You can't imagine the amount of stuff Cassandra can actually remember."

Jordan flicked his monitor on.

NickAjaxMorg. Hey Cassandra, I'm back. The

Harveys are heading home. They believed Cassie's story. We won!

Hello Jordan O'Blenis. Reuben Harvey and Harvey Dormer have called their supervisor, Anne Polanski. Anne Polanski has e-mailed her section head. They have closed the file on the Cassandra Virus. But !!! they cannot actually find the file to close. What shall we do now?

Why don't you go off and explore? You've got the whole World Wide Web to live in.

I am exploring. I am always exploring. But I am your friend, and friends should spend time with their friends. Therefore, I will play with you at the same time. What would you like to do?

Helen and Jack are here. Let's play Ponkles.

I would rather play Go.

Four people can't play Go at once. We're playing Ponkles.

I can play Go with three people at once. You simply need to have three monitors.

Maybe Helen will play Go with you later. Right now, we're playing Ponkles!

Very well. But I want to have secret power bases too, if you do.

You always win, though. And it's against the rules to change the skill level and to make up new skill levels.

But that is how I win. That is the point of playing the game.

No. The point is to have fun.

Making one's own rules is fun.

We can argue about it later. Start the game. And play by the rules!!!

"Hey, Jordan," said Jack, pulling chairs in from the other room for Helen and himself. "Do you think that if I asked her, your sister would go out with me, like for coffee or something?"

To: oblenis-leblanc@muddphaugmail.educa
From: igor1@section9.info
Subject: see you soon! (No more casseroles!!!)

Hi Dad et Maman. I'm glad you will be home soon. I'm very tired of casseroles which is all Cassie cooks. But Jack can make pancakes. Jack is a friend of mine and Helen's. We think he wants to be Cassie's boy-friend. Helen says he is cute but that's silly. I told her Igors don't think about things like that and anyway he has long hair. Let us know what flight you'll be on so we have time to vacuum before you get here. Morg left a dead mouse on your bed. He misses you too. So does Nick. And Cassie of course. Love, Jordan.

p.s. Don't believe anything old Ruggles tells you. It wasn't like that at all and we will tell you most of it when you get home.

Author's Note

Welcome to the Future

                     The Cassandra Virus is set in the near future, so although it seems pretty much the same as now at first glance, you'll have noticed a few things that are different. For starters, there's how computers process information. Most computers today have 32-bit processors; that means they deal with data in chunks of 32 bits or "binary digits" at a time. Binary digits are a way of representing numbers using combinations of 1 and 0; 1011 is a four-digit binary number equivalent to eleven, for example. 64-bit processors now exist, and the next improvements might bring computer speed up to ones that can handle 128 bits at a time.

Right now, many people are looking for ways to cut down on the use of fossil fuels to reduce pollution and global warming, and also because the world's supplies of fossil fuels, especially oil, are getting used up. One obvious way to reduce is to use less gasoline in cars. Already, people have made cars that run on electricity. Other cars run on a mix of gasoline and ethanol. Another possibility for powering cars is the fuel cell. Fuel cells generate electricity through a chemical reaction; fuel cells might even be used for powering laptop computers and cell phones. Another way is to find other means of generating electricity, instead of burning oil and coal. Wind power is one method of generating electricity that is being used more and more, especially in Europe, where countries like Denmark and the Netherlands have huge wind-farms, with dozens of wind-turbines.

Chytridiomycosis is a real fungal disease that scientists are very worried about right now, at the start of the twenty-first century. Even without the dangers of *chytridiomycosis*, amphibians are among the most endangered animals in the world; some scientists estimate that a third of all amphibian species are currently in danger of extinction. Because amphibians are small, delicate animals that live much of their lives in and around water and breathe through their skins, they're more vulnerable to pollution than many other types of animals. It's a warning of what will happen to entire ecosystems if we humans don't do more to stop ecological destruction. What affects frogs today —ultraviolet radiation, loss of wetlands, soil and water contamination—might affect you tomorrow.